Brave Hearts

B.K. Wright

Brave Hearts

Beau to Beau Books
E-mail: info@beautobeau.com
Website: http://www.beautobeau.com
ISBN: 978-1-6184-5215-3
Printed in the United States of America

Table of Contents

King of Hearts

When Marc notices the silhouette of a man who he is certain is the man he had loved many years ago, old feelings come flooding back instantly. When he discovers that this man is, indeed, the man from his past, but who now is holding a baby in his arms, Marc has no idea what to say to him. This man is the only man Marc has ever loved, but with a baby in his arms this man from Marc's past has obviously moved on. When the two of them begin reminiscing about old times, Marc quickly learns that this man he loved so many years ago may hold more than his heart. This man may hold the many secrets and questions surrounding Marc's past.

Marc was sitting with his two teenaged sons when a familiar silhouette suddenly caught his eye. He looked up and thought he saw a man from his past. He was certain that it was Todd. Marc watched as the man walked by, a young child in his arms. It was Todd. Marc knew that it was. He could never forget him. He would never forget him. What had it been, ten years?

"Todd," he shouted.

The man turned around. "Marc, is that you?"

Todd hurried back to where Marc was sitting, just as Marc was standing up. "Oh, my God. How are you?"

Marc threw his arms around the man from his past. "Todd, these are my two boys." Marc introduced his two almost adult sons. Todd didn't say anything about the baby that he was cradling in his arms.

"Is this your daughter?" Marc asked.

"Oh, no. This is Ruthie's baby. Ruthie has four girls now, and she is married to a man she met in college."

Todd looked nervously at Marc's sons. How much did they know about their father? Had Marc told them about him?

"Come on, Dad. We have a game."

"Oh, hey, I can give you a lift; that is, if you want to stay and catch up," Todd offered, a little hesitantly.

"Cool," Marc's oldest son exclaimed. "The keys, please."

Marc reluctantly handed the keys to his jeep over to his sixteen year old son. "I want it back in one piece."

"Thank you for the concern for our safety over your jeep, Dad. It's very heartwarming."

Marc laughed. "See what I get for wishing for sons," he teased.

Todd sat down beside Marc. "So, you baby-sitting, or what?"

"No, just waiting for Ruthie to come back. She has four daughters, but this one is their last, so she is extra spoiled."

"Damn, Todd, I had no idea you were living in Lincoln, Nebraska. What do you do here in Lincoln?"

Todd looked at Marc. "I'm a programmer for the state government."

"Nice, Todd, real nice." "Hey, some government jobs are not nearly as cushy as you may think."

Looking at Todd, Marc felt as if he had stepped back in time. He and Todd seemed to be picking up right where they had left off.

"Don't tell me you moved back here to Lincoln, of all places?" Todd asked, in disbelief. Marc nodded.

"We moved here five years ago. I'm a professor now at the University of Nebraska-Lincoln, good old UNL. I teach Modern and Classical Languages."

"My, big man on campus."

Marc smiled at Todd's comment.

Ruthie came up to them and squealed with delight. "Oh, my God. It's been a long time, Marc. Can you believe I have four kids now, all girls?"

"Good to see you again, kid," Marc said, as Ruthie took her daughter from Todd's arms.

"Oh, I do miss being called kid." She winked and then left with her girls.

"So, tell me, Marc. How's married life?"

Marc looked down. "I'm not married, Todd." "How about you, Todd? Anyone special?"

Todd stared at Marc, not saying a word. "You know the answer to that," he said. "Your memory can't possibly be that bad, at least not yet," he added.

"I know," Marc admitted. Then he looked around, not knowing what to say to Todd after all these years. "Guess I should have left with my boys."

"Oh, shit, Marc. That was ten years ago. Come on. I'll show you my house. I live on a lake now. That's what we do here in the Midwest, you know. We are so landlocked that we have to make our lakes."

"I grew up here, too, you know," Marc reminded him.

Todd gave his old friend a half smile, and the two of them walked in silence to Todd's car.

"The city has grown a lot, and spread out," Marc commented, as they drove through the city, and to Todd's house just outside of the city. Todd nodded in agreement with Marc's comment. There was silence in Todd's car until they reached his house.

"Not bad, Todd. Not bad at all," Marc exclaimed, when he walked into Todd's house.

"I like it," Todd said, and showed Marc around his house.

Marc wasn't at all surprised to have walked into a very well kept house. He picked up a figurine of some sort, and then set it back down. "You always did have great taste, Todd, or is that still, Hot Toddy?"

Todd laughed. "Shit. I haven't been called Hot Toddy since you, Marc."

Marc looked around. "You have a pool, and a lake lot?"

"Sure do. You can save a lot of money when you live alone," Todd said, as he handed his friend a drink.

"Thanks."

Marc looked at Todd. Was that bitterness that he heard in his old friend's voice, or maybe sarcasm?

"Damn, Todd, what is this stuff?"

"It's a wine drink. It is the newest thing in France."

"You have been to France, Todd?"

"Once, but a friend sent me a supply," Todd admitted.

"A friend, huh?"

"That's right." Marc looked out at the lake as he drank the sweet drink.

Marc had almost finished his drink when he felt Todd's hand on his shoulder. "It's beautiful, isn't it?"

Marc turned his head slightly. "Yeah. Guess I never expected this much beauty here in Lincoln."

Todd wrapped his arm around his friend's chest. "Did you expect to see me again?"

Marc ran his hand along his friend's arm. "No, I did not expect this," he admitted, being somewhat evasive in his response.

Marc stood and waited, not knowing what he was waiting for. Marc soon felt his friend's other arm around his waist. Todd lightly brushed his lips against the back of Marc's neck. Marc held onto Todd's arm, the memories of their shared past flooding his mind. Todd brushed his lips along the side of Marc's neck, coming closer and closer to Marc's lips, the lips that Marc could never resist. Todd gently pulled Marc's earlobe into his mouth and held it between his lips. Then he placed his mouth over Marc's ear and whispered, "Better get you home now."

Marc turned instantly and pulled Todd around to where he had been standing. Marc kissed those lips that had been the first ever to have kissed his own. The wine drink made the taste of those lips even better than Marc had remembered. Todd tried to resist Marc, but he could not. In an instant, the old feelings came flooding back to him, too. He forced himself to pull away and to turn his back to Marc.

"Todd?"

"I can't do this, Marc. I will not let myself get pulled into a fantasy."

Marc now stood behind his first love. "Maybe this is not a fantasy."

Todd crossed his arms, but Marc did not leave. Todd could feel Marc behind him. He could feel Marc's hot breath on his neck. Todd stared out at his own pool and at the lake view that he loved. "Why, Marc? Why did you disappear?"

Marc put his arms around Todd, folding them across Todd's chest. He spoke softly, yet distinctly and certainly. "I did not disappear. You knew where I was the entire time. You could have come to me."

Marc looked down at Todd's arms holding him. "I had to stay behind. I had to convince them that what they had seen was not what they had thought it was. I went to their stuffy choice of colleges, our father's alma mater, Creighton University, in dear old Omaha, Nebraska. But you, you got to live the life of the free spirit in Los Angeles."

"Yes," Marc agreed. "I spent ten years studying every one of the liberal arts, living and learning with liberal minds, but I never stopped loving you, wanting you, needing you."

Todd closed his eyes. "I missed you, Marc. You must have married. You have sons."

"Do the math, Todd. I have been gone for ten years, yet the two boys are in their teens."

"Whose are they?"

Marc continued to speak softly and slowly to his first love who continued to face away from him. "I was not celibate all of these years, as I am certain you have not been either. I met a man with two sons. We were together for two years. He was dying. He begged me to adopt his sons, and I did. I love those boys as if they were mine."

Todd's heart was breaking at the thought of Marc loving another man. "Did you love him, Marc, the way you loved...?"

"The way I loved you? No, I did not. I loved him, as I am sure you have loved others. But you know that there is and never will be a love like ours."

Todd could feel Marc's heart beating against his back. He didn't want to give in to old feelings and desires, but he could no longer resist his first lover and his forever love.

Todd turned around and looked at Marc. Todd's eyes were full, as were his lover's. "Marc," he said, and gently held his face. He kissed Marc's lips, touching his face. After one kiss, he stopped. Marc's eyes remained closed, his lips parted, his heated breath pulsing against Todd's lips. Marc slowly opened his eyes, wondering why his lover had stopped kissing him.

"Take me, Todd. Take me like you did so many years ago."

Todd's hand was on Marc's zippered jeans, and he slowly slid the zipper downward along its track. He watched Marc's face as he forced his hard cock and balls out from their denim prison. "Take them off," he ordered.

Marc dutifully obeyed, and removed his jeans. He stood naked from the waist down, his hard cock begging to be touched. Todd held Marc's cock in his hand while he continued to watch

Marc's face. Marc closed his eyes at his lover's touch. Todd reached for Marc's balls, letting his cock slide along his arm. Marc opened his legs for his lover.

"Take this off," Todd ordered, tugging at Marc's shirt. Marc almost tore his shirt off of his body.

With nothing between his naked body and the clear view of the lake with the exception of Todd's body, Marc was completely exposed to anyone who might be walking by the lake. Todd looked at Marc. In his eyes was the look that had been there ten years ago. He slid his hands along the sides of Marc's body, down over his butt, and around to his hips. Todd looked down at Marc's cock for the first time in ten years. He held onto Marc's legs and lowered himself to his knees. His lips were so close to the fullness of Marc's cock that Marc could feel the breath of his lover as it reached the leaking head. Todd looked up. Marc's eyes were closed, and a moan escaped his lips. Todd's tongue on the head of his cock made Marc's legs feel weak. Todd's hands tightened their hold on Marc's legs, and Todd rested Marc's cock on his tongue and then slowly urged it into his mouth. He grabbed onto Marc's butt and slammed Marc's cock into his mouth until Marc was thrusting forcefully.

Todd wrapped his arms tightly around Marc's butt, holding his lover's cock deep within his mouth. Todd gasped. Marc moaned. Todd missed his lover's cock, and Marc missed his lover. The two lovers could have been easily seen from the glass door if anyone had chosen to look, but neither of them cared. Marc steadied himself by holding onto Todd's head. He thrust his cock forward, and Todd eagerly accepted it. Marc's forceful thrusts hit the back of Todd's throat, and Todd squeezed his lover's butt.

"Oh, shit, Todd."

Marc held tighter to Todd's thick head of hair, and forced his cock harder into his lover. When Todd stroked between the two halves of Marc's butt and reached the entrance that no other lover had filled the way that he had, Marc brought Todd's head forcefully to his crotch, and filled his lover with his hot cream.

"Oh, Todd, it's been so long," he moaned. No one had given Todd what Marc had given him. No one's juice was as sweet as Marc's. Todd once again wrapped his arms around Marc's butt, holding the cock that he had longed for in the warmth of his mouth until it had been completely satiated of his love. Todd looked up at Marc.

"Don't let go of me, Todd. I honestly could not stand on my own right now."

Todd wasn't sure if Marc was speaking figuratively or literally, but it made no difference. He could never let go of Marc now. He would not let Marc leave him again.

In his weakened state, Marc was easily lifted over Todd's shoulders. "What the fuck?" Marc dangled helplessly over Todd's broader shoulders, grabbing onto Todd's butt to keep from falling.

"Todd, I'm naked here," he protested, looking out and seeing people down by the lake.

Todd walked to his bedroom and flung his lover onto the bed. Marc hit the bed hard. Todd locked the door of his bedroom, and then stood in perfect view of Marc and unburdened his own hard aching cock from its tight confinement of denim. Marc stared at the first man he had made love to, the first hard cock other than his own that he had ever seen, ever felt, ever tasted, and ever loved. Marc remembered their first time together. Todd had been so gentle, so loving, so erotically pleasing, that Marc had compared that first time and this first lover to every lover since, and all had paled in comparison.

"Todd?" Marc had no idea what he had planned to ask, and he said nothing more.

Todd got on the bed and pulled Marc to him. He pulled Marc's legs up and onto his shoulders.

"Todd, I'm not ready," Marc said.

Todd reached over to where he kept his supplies. The smooth strokes of Todd's fingers were what Marc had remembered.

"Oh, Todd," he moaned. Marc closed his eyes. Todd was a selfless lover. Marc's pleasure was Todd's goal. Marc froze when he felt the head of Todd's hardness enter him. Todd massaged his lover's thighs with smooth yet erotic strokes, and Marc was soon ready and eager for his lover to enter him fully.

"Push it in," Marc urged.

Todd entered his lover slowly, and Marc reached out for him.

"Todd, it's just like…"

"Like before?" Todd asked.

"Yes," Marc replied.

Todd's thrusts became more forceful, more passionate, and he watched as his lover's cock began to respond to his lovemaking. Marc was silent in his complete submission to his lover. He could feel his own climax building once again. Marc grabbed onto the bed.

"T..Todd," he gasped.

Todd watched as Marc's climax was reached and unleashed. Todd then gasped and filled his lover, holding tightly to his lover's legs to steady himself. He looked down at his lover's body which was once again satiated.

Their long awaited lovemaking complete, Todd lay beside his lover. Not knowing what to say to the other, the two men stared at the ceiling.

"You came back five years ago?"

"Yes," Marc replied.

"Why here, Marc? Why did you come back here, to Lincoln, Nebraska?"

Marc wiped the sweat from his forehead. "I came back for you, Todd."

Todd laughed.

Marc turned onto his side. "What the fuck is that for, that laugh?"

"Shit, Marc. You have been here for five years and never once tried to see me. We met by chance today at the mall." Todd laughed again, and Marc hit him hard. Todd grabbed Marc by the wrists, forced him down, and spread his body over him.

Holding Marc's arms down on the bed, he looked at him. His eyes were glassy. He looked angry. Marc quickly defended himself. "Todd, I did try to see you. I had no idea where you worked. You have an unlisted home telephone number, and I had no idea what Ruthie's new last name was, not that she would have helped me find you, anyway. So do not tell me that I have not tried to find you. Look, asshole, do you really think that I would have stayed here, uprooted the boys, gotten a job here, and, well, just stayed here, if I did not have this aching need, this burning desire, to be with my one true love?"

Todd's eyes began to soften. He knew that Marc was right. Why *would* he have stayed? "How did you know that I was still here, Marc? I could have left here years ago."

Marc lowered his eyes, and wondered why Todd had not left and why he had not tried to find him. "Why did you not try to find me, Todd?"

Todd lowered his head, let go of Marc's hands, and wrapped his arms around him. "I wanted to, Marc. It should have been me who had to leave here and make a new life on my own, not you."

Marc slowly put his arms around Todd. "They didn't blame *you*, Todd. It was *me* they blamed. They were going to send me to Boys Town, that magical place that straightened out guys like me. A troubled youth, isn't that what I was labeled? I was the trouble maker, not you. I made you gay, remember? You were the perfect son, their good Catholic son."

"I'm so sorry, Marc. How did you know of their plans?"

"They called me out of school the next day. They had it all set up. They said that if I said one word to you about it, they would send me so far from you that I would never get out of the place. I snuck out of the house that night, out of Lincoln, and hitched my way to Los Angeles. It wasn't easy out there. Believe me, it was not all fun and games. I turned tricks for awhile, blowjobs for a buck, but I never let anyone…well, you know. I never let anyone go where you had gone. I wanted only you inside of me."

Todd held even tighter to his lover.

Marc continued with his life story. "I found other jobs, too, and worked my way through college. Then I met, well, the man who died. Got a couple of great kids, though. Maybe they are one of the reasons I came back here. Who knows?"

Todd couldn't believe how wrong he had been. "All these years I thought you had left because you had wanted to, Marc. They told me that you had wanted to leave. I blamed myself, Marc, and that night. I thought that it was all my fault."

"Get off of me, Todd," Marc shouted.

Todd moved over and off of Marc.

"You dumbass, Todd. You always did think that everything was all about you."

Todd turned onto his side. "What are you talking about?"

"You said you blamed yourself. That makes it about you, does it not?"

"Marc, you are a damned fool."

"When are you going to wake up, Todd? Will you ever put the blame on them? They were far from perfect."

Todd looked down toward the bed. "I know, Marc. I just need to know that I didn't mess you up, you know."

Marc stroked Todd's hair. "You need a haircut," he teased. "No, you did not mess me up, Todd. Since when does loving someone mess them up?"

"Damn it, Marc, I'm serious."

"You loved me, Todd, pure and simple. You loved me, Todd, like no one else has ever loved me since. You know we have a bond like no other. If we let it go too far, then so be it. I never thought that we did take it too far. I have no regrets, Todd. All I have is love, for you."

Marc was silent, and rested his hand on the bed. He played with the threads on the spread. Having said his piece, Marc was tired. He turned onto his stomach and put his arms out over his head.

Todd gently rubbed his back. Then he kissed his back, between his shoulders, and then he kissed each of Marc's shoulders. "I do love you, Marc. I have never been the same without you. You and I were so close. They split us up so that people wouldn't talk, but that made them talk even more. When I left for college, people around here didn't wonder as much about us, and there wasn't as much talk. The attention was all on

Ruthie then, and her perfect boyfriend and now husband. Oh, Marc, if only I had known where you were."

Todd continued to massage and kiss Marc's back.

"That's nice," Marc admitted, as his body relented to Todd's lips and Todd's hands.

"Tell me how you felt that night, Todd."

"That night was perfect, Marc. I had loved you for so long, and when you came to me with that look in your eyes, I knew. I knew that it was just you and me, that it had always been just you and me. I held you. I kissed your lips. I stroked your sweet butt which you parted for me and only me."

Todd's hand was now on Marc's butt again, and Marc parted his legs just as he had that night. "You wanted me inside you, and I wanted to be inside you. I wanted you to feel good, to feel pleasure, to feel love." Todd began to stroke his lover with his long fingers, deeply and erotically. Marc moved just a little to make room for his cock made hard by his lover's touch. Marc began to move with Todd. "How could something so beautiful be considered so wrong?"

Marc turned onto his back, forcing his lover's finger out of him. He pulled Todd to him. "It *is* beautiful, Todd. There is nothing wrong about it or about us. Marc kissed Todd's lips and stroked his back. "You are hard again, Todd."

"Yes," he said, and kissed Marc passionately and longingly.

Todd broke the kiss and looked at Marc. He turned around and fed his lover, as he took his lover. Todd kneaded his lover's warm flesh and devoured his manhood. He made love to Marc's cock, and Marc made love to Todd's beautiful cock. Their lovemaking reached its simultaneous pinnacle, and once again they drank of the juice of the other.

Todd lay beside his lover. "How could that be wrong, what we just did, what we just made?" Todd asked of his lover.

Marc had no argument. They slept together on Todd's bed for just a little while.

"Todd, what time is it?" Marc asked frantically when he awoke. "I need to get home to the boys, Todd."

Todd was on his feet and met Marc midway to the door of his bedroom. "Where do we go from here, Marc? I cannot live another ten years without you. I *will* not live another ten years without you."

Marc stood still, Todd's hands on his arms. "I know."

"Is it the boys?" Todd asked.

"No. It's not the boys. They are two great kids, and I am a good father to them."

"I'm sure you are, Marc. No one is doubting your ability to parent. What then, Marc? You came here for me, and here I am."

"They will find out, Todd. They will know that we are together. We cannot hide forever."

Todd began to speak, but Marc stopped him. "I know they cannot do anything to me now. I am an adult. But my boys are not. Those two sweet young men would not understand the hatred and rejection that they would be met with, and I will not subject those two sweet boys to them and their closed minds."

Todd was impressed with Marc's protectiveness.

"What? Why are you looking at me like that?"

"I am impressed with you, Marc. You would do anything to protect your boys."

The two men stared at each other, not caring, or maybe forgetting, that they were completely naked. "Yes, Todd, I would kill for those boys," Marc said, and Todd knew by the determined look in his eyes that he had meant it.

Todd looked down, realized that he was completely naked, and began to put his clothes on.

"That's it, Todd? That's all that you have to say?"

"Why don't we get dressed, Marc?"

"Fine," Marc said. Once dressed, Marc began to walk toward the door of the bedroom.

"Marc, wait."

Marc stopped at the door of the bedroom and turned around. He leaned on the side of the door, his arms crossed. "What?"

"They're gone, Marc, both of them."

Marc squinted his eyes for a brief second, forming a look of disbelief on his face. "Where did they go, the South of France? Was the shame too much for them to bear? Were the neighbors giving them looks of shame or worse, looks of blame?"

"Marc, don't."

"Don't what? I have no feelings for them. They sent me away. They rejected me, Todd. They rejected me for who I was. They rejected the child that supposedly they had chosen to bring into their home." Marc looked down. "And they rejected you, too, Todd. They didn't want you around either, did they?"

"No, Marc, they did not. We spoke rarely after you left. They refused to talk about it, any of it."

"So how can you defend that bitch and that bastard?"

"I do not defend them, Marc. But, I think...."

"What, Todd, tell me, what do you think?"

Todd looked beaten down. "I just stopped thinking about them. When I said they were gone, I meant that they are dead, Marc. They were killed in a head-on car crash six years ago."

Marc slid slowly down the side of the door until he was sitting on the floor. He rested his head on the side of the door and looked at Todd. Todd's head was down. He couldn't look at Marc. Marc's sobs broke the silence in the room. Todd slowly walked over to the door and sat on the floor. He pulled Marc to him and held him.

"Talk to me, Marc."

Marc lifted his head and through his tear stained face he looked at Todd. "Why am I crying? Why do I even care?"

Todd held Marc's hands. "Because death is the final reality, I suppose. Somewhere in a remote corner of your mind, maybe on the subconscious level even, there was until now a tiny sliver of hope that you would at least have a chance of reconciling with them."

Marc looked at Todd. "But I hated them, and I still do. I never cared about reconciliation."

"I realize that, Marc, but maybe on some level you at least thought that one day you would have an explanation for their actions."

"Shit, I knew why they did it. I didn't need an explanation. I am not stupid, Todd."

Marc started to get up, but Todd held him down. "I know you are not stupid, Marc. I never said that you were. But, come on, you have had a lot more education than I have had, and in the liberal arts, too. So, you have to know that we are emotional beings, and maybe that's it. Maybe I should have said that it was more on an emotional level, you know, *that* part of your mind, that needed some type of 'closure'."

Marc was trying to tune Todd out, but was not having much luck. "How is Ruthie doing without them?"

"Ruthie took it real hard. She was married though, and in between babies. I think that was when Ruthie went from being a whiny little princess to a grown woman. Her girls were asking questions, and Ruthie had to be strong for them and show them that life does go on. I think her husband had a long talk with her about that and made her see that her moping was hurting her girls. Frank is a straight shooter, and exactly what Ruthie needed."

"She barely spoke to me at the mall today, Todd. Does she blame me, too?"

"No, Marc. She just doesn't understand. She is so much younger than we. She was not a part of us. They called her a 'change of life' baby because they didn't think that they could become pregnant at their age."

"Did you tell her about us?"

"Not really, but you can. Ruthie is a neat kid, Marc. She and Frank are both neat kids. And you will love her girls."

"What am I supposed to tell her, Todd, that the love of my life is you?"

"You do know that we are not blood relatives, don't you?"

"In their eyes it was still wrong."

"Why and how is it wrong?"

"My parents took you in because they were told that you were all alone in the world. You came to us when you were most vulnerable, after your parents had died, remember? We loved each other. The bond between us has never been broken, not by time, not by distance, not by the unknown."

Marc knew that Todd was right, but he suddenly felt tired, very tired. "They thought that I had somehow 'turned you gay', didn't they?"

"Maybe, but when they discovered the truth about me, their only son, their legacy, they couldn't bear it. They blamed themselves, Marc, not you, and they never forgave themselves for what they did to you."

"Bullshit. They never felt any remorse."

"Yes, Marc, they did. I overheard Mom calling information for somewhere on the East Coast one day. They had no idea where to look to find you, and I don't know how many places they called."

"I never had a phone in my name, Todd. I was in school for years, and then I lived with the father of my two boys in his house."

Marc sighed, a deep heavy sigh. "I guess we all have our crosses to bear," he said, looking up at Todd. "But they made me feel loved, until that day."

"I know, Marc. Maybe that is all that we can expect from anyone, really. Maybe that's what life is all about, making those around us feel loved, somehow. Anyway, it's all said and done now."

Marc looked at Todd and shook his head. "You are a just a real King of Hearts, now aren't you?"

"No, Marc, I am just a person."

Under his breath, Marc said, "But you are the King of my Heart."

"Where do we go from here, Todd?"

"Wherever you want us to go, Marc, but I hope that you choose to stay here with me."

"What else *can* I do? You are the only person who has ever made me feel loved, somehow. You are my King of Hearts."

Todd held the man who had shared so much with him and who was the only man he had ever loved. This man who he had considered to be his brother knew him better than he knew himself. "I promise you, Marc, that we will always be together, and I promise you that we will always love, somehow." Marc held tightly to the man who was holding him and to the man he had always loved, knowing that their love was beautiful and right and he knew, too, that they would always love, somehow.

The Company Dad Kept

Maxwell Turner has spent a lifetime building a company that his son will one day inherit, and he has spent his son's lifetime keeping a secret from him. Maxwell is gay and has been living with the love of his life for the past three years, a man who gave up everything to be with him, and the one man Maxwell could never live without. When Maxwell's son discovers that his father is gay, he vows to rid the company that is rightfully his of every "fag", beginning with his own father. Distraught by his son's attitude, Maxwell regrets having kept his secret all these years and is now faced with decisions he is not prepared to make.

Maxwell Turner enjoyed his morning coffee in the bright sunshine as he relaxed on his deck overlooking the lake. He had recently sold his much too spacious home in the country and moved to a smaller, one and a half story patio home in the suburbs, closer to the city, so that he could be closer to his business, his favorite restaurants, and the gym where he now worked out almost daily. Max had worked hard for years growing his business which now enjoyed its rightful place in the Fortune 500. He had entertained many clients at his country estate and had hosted many parties there, but now was ready and very willing to turn over the reins to his son. Now Maxwell spent approximately twenty hours a week at the office instead of the sixty to eighty hours he had previously. His son, Nick, was coming home today, having graduated from Oxford University in England. Nick had been well prepared to run a billion dollar corporation such as Turner Tech Group, and Maxwell was eager to turn over the family business to the next generation. Nick had not been home for three years, and Max was looking forward to his arrival.

Maxwell was greeted by a kiss as he was joined on the deck. "Good morning, Max. What time does Nick's plane come in?"

"Three this afternoon."

"I will make one of my gourmet meals then."

"That would be wonderful. Thank you."

Just then the phone rang, and Maxwell went inside to answer it. He returned to the deck and said, "Well, Nick's arrival couldn't have come at a better time. I need to go to the office for a little while. If Nick calls, tell him I'll pick him up at the airport."

"Will do, and I will see you later."

"I'll stop by before I leave for the airport," Max assured.

The drive to the office was twenty minutes now instead of the all too familiar hour and a half that Max had driven for too long. He was one of the lucky ones and he knew it. Nick's mother had died when Nick was very young, so Nick had been spared the knowledge of his father's unhappiness. Max had had a few relationships during Nick's formative years, but he had been very discreet. It wasn't until Nick had left for college that Max had found the love of his life. The past eight years had been the best years of Maxwell's life. He had met someone on a vacation, but the two of them had kept their relationship a secret from Nick at Max's request. For the past three years, however, the two of them had been living together in this beautiful place on the lake that was now their home.

As Maxwell sat at his desk looking over the reports that needed his approval, he wondered if he had done the right thing by not telling Nick. "It's too late now," he said to no one. Nick would meet the love of his life very soon. Max hurried through his reports, and then rushed home to see his love one more time before going to the airport.

"Mm, smells good in here," Max said, as he walked into the kitchen.

"This is a very special night, Max."

"Yes it is, Chauncey, yes it is," Max agreed. Max kissed Chauncey, and left for the airport.

The airport was busy, as it always was, and Max parked his car and hurried inside to wait for Nick. He was nervous, and he now wished that he had told his son about Chauncey. Max had spent a lifetime keeping his secret in an effort to shield his son from the slings and arrows that would have surely come his way had his friends and classmates known that his father was gay. He had not kept his secret solely to protect his son. He had also kept his secret to protect the family business. Max knew that some of the clients he had invited to his home were gay, but they weren't trying to protect the one thing that Max had worked so hard to build to give to his son. Still, when Max had met Chauncey, his life had changed overnight. Chauncey had waited patiently for Max, seeing him every other month when Max could get away, and their friendship had grown into love over the years despite the distance between them. Chauncey's willingness to sell his own business and uproot his life for Max had been a wonderful gift. Chauncey had been a wonderful gift, and Max wanted nothing more than to share his happiness with Nick.

"There he is. There's my boy," Max exclaimed, as he hugged his son.

"Hey, Dad. It's been awhile."

They had seen each other only via webcam, and the hug had felt good. Nick looked behind him and smiled at a young lady who was hurrying to catch up with him.

"Dad, this is Kate. We met at school. I guess I should have said something, but I've been so busy with school and all."

"I understand. It's nice to meet you, Kate."

Kate shook Maxwell's hand, and she and Nick walked hand in hand to the car.

"It's good to be home, Dad. The city looks the same. Not much changed in the last three years, huh?"

Max smiled to himself. "Oh, a few things have changed, but not that much."

"Well, I guess I should tell you. Kate and I have been living together for awhile now. She's from Philly."

"Well, welcome to Boston, Kate. The two of you were practically neighbors, but had to meet across the pond."

Kate laughed at Max's remark.

"Kate graduated last year, Dad, in finance."

"That's good. I know just the company for her."

"Nick has told me how hard you worked, Mr. Turner. I really admire that."

"Well, that's what you do when you're young and energetic, Kate, and call me Max, please."

"Okay, thanks."

They pulled into the driveway, and Nick looked at the much smaller home. It was a bit of a shock to not be at the old country estate he had grown up at, but this was what his dad had wanted.

"This is nice, Dad, it really is. I like it."

Nick missed the old home, but kept his feelings to himself. Things had changed, and he had no right to tell his father how to live his life, not after he had raised him by himself and had worked so hard. Before they went inside, Nick said, "Dad, if you don't mind, Kate and I thought we would stay at a hotel suite until we moved into a house. That's okay, right?"

"Of course it is. You're a grown man now, and I just have to accept the fact that my baby boy is all grown up," he teased, and pinched Nick's cheek.

Kate giggled. She liked Max. Nick was a lot like him.

"Well, come on in," Max said, and Nick and Kate walked in.

"Something smells good, Dad," Nick said, as Chauncey came from the kitchen.

"This is Chauncey, an old buddy of mine," Max said, as he made the introductions. "Chauncey is a chef."

"It sure smells like it," Nick said, and Kate followed Chauncey back into the kitchen.

"I love to cook. Let me help."

"My first student," Chauncey exclaimed. He was such a fun loving, jolly man, it was no wonder they had clicked. He was a nice complement to Max's more serious nature. Nick and Max joined Kate and Chauncey in the kitchen, and Nick and Kate got things ready for them to eat on the beautiful deck off the kitchen.

"So, looks like Nick has got him someone too," Chauncey said quietly to Max.

"Might soften the blow," Max said.

"He'll be fine, Max, just wait and see."

Max had his doubts, but he wasn't going to bring it up tonight. The four of them had a wonderful dinner, and they all agreed that Chauncey was an excellent chef. Nick and Kate didn't stay very long. They were tired, and were going house hunting first thing in the morning.

"I'll be back, Chauncey," Kate promised, as the two of them left.

After they had left, Chauncey turned to Max and hugged him. "I love you," he said, and kissed Max.

"Mm, you know what I like," Max said.

"Oh, yeah, what is it that you like?" Chauncey teasingly asked, as he pulled Max even closer holding his tight butt in his hands.

Max put his hands on Chauncey's ass. "All of this back here is what I like," Max said, as he squeezed Chauncey's bountiful butt. Chauncey was a big man and Max loved every inch of him. Kate had left her purse in the kitchen and was waiting in the living room, having heard the two of them when she walked in.

"Knock, knock," she said, pretending to have just come in the door. "Forgot my purse." She then walked into the kitchen, having given the two of them time to know that she was there. "The food was so good, I guess I must have lost my head," she said, and smiled sweetly.

They heard the door close, and the car pull out of the driveway. Max sat down. "Damn, you don't think she heard anything, Chauncey?"

"No, it sounded to me like she just came in," he said.

"I guess so," Max agreed, wishing more and more that he had told Nick years ago. But how did a father "come out" to his son, he wondered.

"Come on, Max, take me to bed," Chauncey said, and took Max by the hand. Max loved Chauncey and could never let him go, not now, not even for Nick.

Chauncey led Max to the bed they had shared every night for the last three years and laid him down. Chauncey took off his own clothes and then treated himself to Maxwell's gorgeous well toned body as he undressed him as well. He kissed Max's lips and ran his hands along his chest and then kissed his chest and down to his navel, kissing it, and stroking Max's inner thighs with his meaty hands. Max spread his legs wide for his man. Chauncey wasn't afraid to love. Chauncey had taken Max every way imaginable, and Max had never left their bed unsatisfied. Chauncey was between Max's legs now, moving them apart further, as he helped himself to Max's body.

One touch from Chauncey and Max's body responded with complete submission. "That's my lover," he said, and placed his big thick tongue between Max's legs, holding his butt cheeks apart. Chauncey forced his warm wet tongue between Max's butt cheeks so that the very tip could tease Max's hole.

"Ohh," Max groaned, as he always did when Chauncey played with his hole. He entered Max with just the tip of his tongue before moving upward, pressing on the satiny smoothness beneath Max's balls which caused the first drop to show itself at the very tip of Max's penis. Max moaned for this most giving lover, and enjoyed the senses that Chauncey was awakening in him once again. Chauncey lifted each of Max's heavy cum filled balls onto his thick flat tongue and into his moisture filled mouth.

"Mmm," he hummed, causing more drops to fall on Max's skin. "I've not been good to my Max," Chauncey said, as he lifted the other ball. "They should never be allowed to get this heavy. We wouldn't want an unexpected explosion."

Max loved Chauncey's humor, even in bed. Chauncey moved up and with one sudden movement took Max's cock in its entirety into his mouth and all the way down into his throat. "Oh," Max moaned. His hard penis was throbbing inside Chauncey's mouth and Chauncey began to squeeze it with his mouth as he took it in and then let it out part way, over and over.

"Oh, Chauncey, I love you so much," Max moaned.

Chauncey played with Max's balls as he sucked Max's dick, and Max's climax began to build. Chauncey was the most uninhibited lover Max had ever had. There wasn't any part of Max that had not had the pleasure of Chauncey's mouth, lips, hands, or dick. The way he loved made Max lose the many inhibitions of his years before Chauncey. He was a gentle lover, yet left no part of Max unsatisfied. Chauncey moved to Max's side, taking his hardness in his mouth. He held Max's butt and rolled it upward to bring Max's beautiful cock into his mouth. Before Chauncey, Max would have felt uncomfortable with his ass pointed skyward, but not now, not with Chauncey. Chauncey had total control over Max's body when they were making love. Chauncey had positioned Max's body in various ways, each time bringing Max to an orgasmic release he would never have thought possible. Chauncey held Max's legs with his strong arms, opening Max's butt cheeks with his fingers and playing with Max's hole. He sucked forcefully on Max's hard rod, making slurping noises which caused Max to moan and his dick to provide Chauncey with drop after drop of the best sauce in the house, as Chauncey had put it.

"Mm, mm," Chauncey would say with every drop, and Max would open his legs for him, as he enjoyed every minute of lovemaking with Chauncey. "You've got a lot for me today, don't you baby?" Chauncey said, as he squeezed Max's heavy balls.

"Mm, hmm," Max said, almost there already.

Chauncey slid a finger into his mouth along Max's shaft to wet it and also to bring more pleasure to Max. Max gasped when he felt Chauncey's finger along the smooth space beneath his balls and on down to where he placed it firmly over the entrance to Max's inner space that Chauncey could fill like no other man had. When Chauncey was inside him, he would always bring Max to a second climax, emptying whatever was left inside his once heavy balls. Max began to thrust toward Chauncey, and Chauncey held Max's delicious ass with one hand to make Max's thrusts stronger and his coming orgasm more powerful, and with the other hand Chauncey held Max's ass cheeks apart as he entered him deeply with his wetted finger. Chauncey's fingers were meaty and very filling as he brushed Max's inner pleasure with smooth strokes. Chauncey sucked hard on Max's hardness and with strong thrusts as he eagerly awaited the release of that yummy sauce that had been kept warm and prepared just for him within Max's heavy balls. He knew that Max had been stressed about Nick's arrival, and Chauncey was just the man to give him everything he needed.

"Mm, that's it, baby, give it to Chauncey," he said. He opened Max a little more with another of his beefy fingers, and felt a short burst of Max's sauce shoot out from the spongy head that was deep inside his throat. Chauncey stroked Max deep inside and another burst shot forth. "Yum. I'm ready for more now," Chauncey encouraged, and Max moaned loudly as a strong burst of cum left his balls and entered Max. "Mm, hmm," Chauncey said, knowing that Max had begun to get the release he needed. Chauncey continued, and Max had two more bursts for him before he couldn't give any more. Chauncey held Max against him and continued to suck until Max's hardness began to retreat. He slowly withdrew his fingers and lowered Max's legs down to the bed. He kept Max's legs apart and got between them, looking up at Max. His eyes were closed, and little beads of sweat glistened in the hair on his chest. Chauncey lifted Max by his cute well toned butt and wiggled his tongue into his entrance. Max gasped, and Chauncey playfully wiggled his tongue in further, lightly touching the interior walls and leaving a trail of Max's cum as he withdrew. "Oh," Max moaned, and held his soft dick that was already showing the first signs of hardness again. "I think my baby has some more sauce in there," Chauncey said, as he swiped each of Max's balls with his tongue. Then he licked Max's hand that was holding his cock. Chauncey kneaded Max's buns with his hands and licked beneath Max's balls and then entered him again with his tongue, this time all the way in. "Ohh," Max moaned, as he stroked his cock. "That sweet sauce is going to be mine very soon," Chauncey said, with passion and confidence. He teased Max's hole with the head of his dick before flipping Max's relaxed body over. He had Max into position, and lifted his sweet hole to his tongue again. "Uh, oh Chauncey," Max moaned.

Max was well prepared before Chauncey entered him, and was also hard again. Chauncey stopped just long enough to line Max's interior with the most erotic lube ever made which never failed to cause a drop of cum to fall onto the bed. "Mm, did it again," Chauncey said, and another drop followed. He inched the head of what Max called his love stick into Max and ran his hands along Max's back as he entered him. Max lifted his ass to Chauncey eagerly.

"Just look at that sweet ass," Chauncey said, as he fondled it. He pulled out part way and then entered again. He continued at a steady pace as he entered Max again and again. He reached below Max and held his erect penis in his hand and let it slide against the palm as he entered Max. Max began a steady moan, and Chauncey felt the steady drip of cum in his hand from Max's hardness. Chauncey licked Max's butt cheeks with gentle swipes on each side. He slid his hands along Max's back again, massaging as he entered him.

"Max, I'm getting close, baby. You are so good to me," Chauncey said with passion. "I'm going to fill you tonight, baby. You've got more sauce for me, too, don't you?"

"Mm," Max said.

Chauncey sped up his pace and went deep inside Max with every thrust, gently holding Max's penis in his hand. "That's it," Chauncey moaned, as Max thrust backward against Chauncey's forward movements. Chauncey thrust and moaned, and stroked the rest of Max's cum from inside the warmth of his balls, as his own full load of cum opened Max's ass and made room for its own arrival. "Oh, that's my baby. That's what Chauncey wanted."

Max's cum released into Chauncey's hand, and Max's balls were now completely empty. Chauncey pulled Max's legs straight and lay over him with his legs on either side of Max's and his arms over Max's. He kissed Max's cheek and then his neck, and rested his head on Max's back. The sweat from his chest mingled with the sweat on Max's back, and Chauncey loved it. He loved the smell of their love. It had taken Max a little time to get used to Chauncey's spontaneity, and he had also had to fight the urge to shower before and after sex, but Chauncey had taught him that love was not something that was planned. Chauncey wanted Max when he was in his most natural state, especially when he was just waking up. He kissed Max on the back and massaged his sweaty armpits.

"I love you, Max, my hot sexy lover."

He slid his hands underneath Max and placed them flat over his nipples, and fell asleep just as they were, his now soft penis still snug inside of Max. The low steady sound of Max's snoring lulled him to sleep.

The alarm went off the next morning and Max reached out and pushed the button. "Now this is the way to wake up," Chauncey said, still on him and still in him. He turned Max's head and kissed him on the lips. "Morning, baby," he said. He kissed his neck with slow kisses. Max was already hard. The very touch of Chauncey excited him now. No seduction was necessary, though Max didn't mind at all. He loved Chauncey, and felt lucky to have him. Max thrust up against Chauncey, whose rod was still inside him and hard again.

"Mm, you've got something for me, baby?"

"I might," Max teased.

Chauncey reached underneath Max and found what he wanted. "There it is. Time to go, buddy." He stroked Max and thrust his penis inside him, as if they had never stopped last night. Almost every morning began like this, and Max loved the feel of this man in him and on him. They both came together in the mornings, and this morning was no different. Chauncey pulled out of Max, and kissed both sides of his gorgeous ass before going to the kitchen to start the coffee.

Max showered first since he had to go to the office. It was a big day today. Max was introducing the new head of Turner to its board of directors. He kissed Chauncey and headed out the door.

Nick was meeting him at the office, and he pulled into his new parking space right after Max. "There he is, my son, the captain of this ship," Max said, as he hugged Nick. "Where did you leave that pretty little girl of yours?"

"Kate is going house shopping this morning. She'll be here for the lunch with the board, though."

"Good. Well, let's go up to the office. We've got a lot to do before we meet with the board."

Nick followed Max up to his office. He was lucky to be starting at the top of the corporate ladder, but he was also starting at the top of the responsibility ladder, too. Max had raised him to be independent and to think for himself, so felt confident that Nick could handle it. They drank a cup of coffee and then Max went over the responsibilities of the board members and the top executives. Nick looked at the sheets on each member and each executive. Max watched as Nick studied each one.

"The personal information on some of these employees intrigues me, Dad."

"Why is that, Nick?"

"Well, like these two, same address, come on, Dad, I'm not stupid. And, here are two more. This one is questionable, if you know what I mean."

Max was stunned at Nick's comments. "What do you mean, Nick?"

"Let me make myself clear, Dad. There will be no place for fags in my company."

"With all due respect, son, Turner Tech Group is not your company. It is still mine."

"A matter of time and paperwork, Dad, that's all."

"These men and women have been with me for a long time, Nick, and they know this company inside and out."

"Well, Dad, this company is now a fag-free one."

Max was mad now. "How dare you, Nick. I built this company one day at a time, with the help of these people. Need I remind you that this company put you through college?"

"Shit, Dad, why so sensitive? I want good people here, too, just not fags."

"Do you know many gays, Nick?"

Nick squirmed in his chair. "No, fortunately, I don't, and I don't want to know any if I can help it."

"Excuse me for a minute, son," Max said, and walked down the hall. He needed to get away from Nick for awhile. He couldn't understand where his attitude came from. Should I have told him years ago? He is rejecting who I am. Max nearly bumped into a door, but was stopped by one of his so called "fag" execs.

"Hey, Max, you okay?"

"Oh, yeah, thanks Stan. I guess I wasn't watching where I was going."

"Come talk to me if you like," he offered.

"Thanks, Stan."

Max walked down to the coffee shop and sat for a few minutes as he thought about what had just happened up in his office. Stan walked in and bought a cup of coffee and was on his way out when he saw Max sitting alone in a corner of the coffee shop staring out the window. Stan had been Max's right hand for many years. He sat down in the chair opposite Max's.

"Hey, Max. Now I know something is wrong. First, you almost run into a door, and now you're sitting alone staring out the window."

Max brushed back his hair. "Oh, Stan, I've really done it this time," he admitted.

"It can't be that bad. Let me help."

"Stan, I'm canceling the meeting today and Nick's introduction. I need to talk to him, man to man."

"Gotcha. You do what you need to do, Max, and I'll take care of things around here, cancel the meeting and the lunch, okay?"

Max sighed. "Thanks, Stan. Thanks for everything."

Max stood up and hugged his long time friend. "Tell Frank I said he's got himself a good one," he said, and Stan blushed. Max went back to his office.

"I've been looking over more of the personnel files, Dad, and you could save a bundle right here," Nick said with enthusiasm.

"How's that?" "Right here, Dad. You are giving your fag couples health insurance like you do married couples. That will stop right now. And, I plan to double the premiums of the gay singles. Too much of a drain on the company's resources."

Max felt the beginnings of a headache. "Nick, how do you know if a person is gay?"

"Starting now, Dad, they have to tell and if they do things that indicate otherwise, they will be fired."

Max glared at Nick.

"And you know, Dad, I didn't want to say anything, but last night your friend, Chauncey, was looking at you in a funny way. I'd watch him if I were you."

That was the last straw. Nick would not talk about Chauncey. "Nick, the meeting and the lunch have been cancelled."

"Oh, what's wrong, Dad, are you sick? Go on home, and I'll take over right now."

"Come with me, Nick, and leave those files," Max ordered.

"Sure, Dad, what's up?"

"Just keep walking," Max said.

They walked out the door of the lobby, and Max told Nick to get into his car with him. "Where are we going, Dad?" Max said nothing, but drove to his home sweet home that he shared with the love of his life.

"Did you forget something, Dad?"

"Yes, Nick, apparently I did. I don't know where you got that holier than thou attitude of yours, but there is no place for it in my company or in my life."

"Hey, Dad, it's not about you. I just have different views."

"It is about me, Nick. For years, I did everything I could to shield you from life's pains, especially after your mom died. But your attitude is hurting me. Do you know why I never remarried, or brought a woman home?"

Nick thought for a minute. "No, I guess I never really thought about it. Guess I thought you missed Mom so much you didn't want anyone else."

"No, Nick, that isn't it. Your mom and I were never very happy, but you were too young to know that. Nick, what I shielded you from was me. I'm gay, Nick."

Max's heart was beating fast now and he wished that he was in Chauncey's arms. Nick stared at Max.

"So, I guess all those parties you had with your 'clients' were just one big orgy. Life is just one big fucking orgy, isn't it, Dad?"

"Nick, you will not talk to me like that. I have never had an orgy. I have been with Chauncey now for eight years. He gave up everything for me. He sold his restaurant, his house, gave up everything he had on the West Coast to move across the country and to the cold harsh winters of Boston so I could prepare my company for my ungrateful narrow minded son," Max shouted.

Nick just stared at Max.

"And when you wanted to go to Oxford to get a third degree that you really didn't need, just wasn't ready to work for a living, I agreed and paid for it, and continued to bust my ass at a very stressful job that I was ready to give to you then."

Nick felt sick, but not with remorse. He felt sick thinking about his dad with Chauncey, in bed.

Nick laughed. "My dad's a fag," he laughed.

"Don't you laugh at me. Don't you dare laugh at me."

Kate pulled up beside them then and knew something was wrong. They didn't even notice her. She hurried to the door of the house and knocked, but then walked in.

"Chauncey?"

"Oh, hi, Kate."

"Chauncey, something is wrong. Max and Nick are sitting out front yelling at each other. But before you go out there, I need to tell you something. When I came back for my purse last night, I heard you and Max talking, you know, like lovers, but I didn't say anything to Nick. I'm happy for you, but Nick won't be. He did some bad things in England to gays, and if that's what Max is telling him, about you two, I don't know what's going to happen. I'm sorry."

Chauncey hugged Kate. "Would you watch things on the stove for me, babe?"

"Sure," she said.

Chauncey opened the door to find Nick pulling Max out of the car forcefully. "That company is mine, you faggot. I will rid that place of every one of its faggots, starting with you."

Chauncey pulled Nick away from Max and held him by the arms.

"Let go of me you faggot," Nick screamed.

Max was sobbing now as he stumbled out of the car.

"Max, go on in, and tell Kate to take Nick home."

Max walked into the house.

"I'm sorry, Mr. Turner, I really am," Kate said.

Max nodded.

"Tell Chauncey I put everything on simmer," she said, and walked out the door.

"Nick, let's go. I'm leaving now, so if you don't want to walk, it's now."

Nick turned around and spat on Chauncey before going with Kate. Chauncey waited until Kate pulled out of the driveway before going back inside.

He turned everything off on the stove, and went to the bedroom. Max was still, not a sound from him. Chauncey went back to the kitchen and called Stan at the office. He knew he could trust Stan, and knew that Max trusted Stan.

"Oh, no," Stan said. "I will have security at every door, and not allow Nick in. Keep me posted."

Max thanked Stan, and went to be with Max. He lay on the bed beside Max and stroked his hair. Max's eyes were open and seemed to be fixed on nothing in particular. Chauncey said nothing. Words weren't what Max needed right now. What Max needed now he was getting, his partner's touch. Max continued to stare at nothing, and Chauncey continued to stroke his hair. Max closed his eyes, and Chauncey thought that he was sleeping. He opened his eyes and the tears streamed down his face. Chauncey pulled Max's body to him and held him snugly against his big warm body in his big strong arms. Max buried himself in Chauncey's body, in its warmth, in its love, thankful to have him. Max's body was shaking, and Chauncey held him tightly. The vision of Max's own son eager to physically harm this dear sweet man he now held in his arms caused the tears to form in Chauncey's eyes and drop one by one onto Maxwell's black hair with its streaks of light silver. Chauncey had seen how hard Max had worked to ready the company he had built for his son. Chauncey knew the toll the long hours had taken on Max. Chauncey held Max while he slept. Max was tired, exhausted really, though it was not yet noon. After about an hour, Maxwell awoke and pushed back to look at Chauncey.

"Guess I dozed off. What time is it?"

"It's a little past noon, baby. Go ahead and sleep, Max," Chauncey said firmly.

"No, I'm okay. I need to call Stan."

"Look, Max, I never interfere, but I did call Stan after Nick left because Kate filled me in on a few things and I didn't want Nick to cause problems while you were here and not at the office."

"Oh, okay, thank you, I mean it, thanks."

"I still need to talk to Stan, though."

"Well, baby, why don't I call Stan and have him come here. I think you need to stay right where you are and let me take care of you," Chauncey offered, as he took off Max's shoes and tucked him underneath the covers.

"Thanks," Max said, and Chauncey kissed him on the cheek.

Max slept the rest of the afternoon, and Stan came by after work. The three of them sat in the living room. Max kept no secrets from Chauncey. He knew what Max was going to do.

"Hey, Max, you don't look so good, boss." Stan hugged Max as he said this. The two of them had been through a lot in the past twenty-some years. "What can I do for you?"

Max told Stan everything that Nick had said, everything he had planned to do with the company, and how things had gone here at the house. Chauncey was as surprised as Stan by Nick's attitude toward gays. They both had thought that Nick was just upset with his father. Stan pulled Max to him and hugged him again.

"I'm so sorry. I knew you were going through something this morning. How can I help?"

"Stan, you've been with me all the way with the company, and you know the company inside and out. I want you to take my place, Stan. Everyone loves you and trusts you. You will offer equality and fairness to all who work there. Nick could not do that. He was going to change the philosophy on which the company was founded. I couldn't let him do that."

Stan took Max's hand. "I humbly accept, Max. You will retain a seat on the board, right?"

"Yes, Stan, I'll still be around. I just can't keep working like I have been. You're ten years younger than I and have a vibrancy about you that will only strengthen the company. It's better this way, for me to step down when the company is strong. You do understand, don't you, Stan?"

"I do, Max, I do. You and Chauncey can take that cruise now that you've always wanted to take. Don't put that off."

"We won't, Stan, we won't," Max assured him, looking at Chauncey.

"I hate to bring it up so soon, but about Nick, where do we stand?"

"Nick is probably long gone by now, but he will have no place in the company. He still has his trust fund and plenty of money, a good education. He will be fine."

Stan stood up and walked toward the door.

"Could you have everything ready for me to sign next week?"

"Of course I can. You two going somewhere for a few days?"

Max looked at Chauncey. "I'm up for it," he said.

"Take good care of him, Chauncey," Stan said, and left the two of them alone.

"Where shall we go?" Chauncey asked, his eyes dancing.

"Let's fly to New York for a couple of days. I thought we'd see a play, and stop in at a jewelry store, Max offered."

Chauncey was out of his chair in a second and sitting beside Max, one leg over him, as if he were trying to sit in his lap. He took Max's face in his hands and kissed his lips, kissing, kissing, holding his mouth open with his own, until Max could barely breathe. Chauncey reluctantly pulled his mouth off of Max's and kissed his neck, while Max focused on catching his breath.

"Does this mean what I think it does?" "Yes," Max said, smiling.

"Yes, it does."

"I will make you the happiest man in the world," Chauncey promised, and then had his mouth back on Max's before he could say a word. He kissed Max's cheek and whispered in his ear, "I can satisfy any sexual fantasy you may have, my love."

Max felt the familiar stirrings that he always did when he was near Chauncey. "I know you can," he said, and put his arms around Chauncey.

"I will have you in bed before and after the show," he whispered, and nibbled Max's earlobe.

Max's arousal was going to be very obvious very soon if Chauncey didn't stop talking like that, Max thought, but held him even closer.

The next morning they were on a company jet to New York City. They were staying in the heart of Manhattan in a suite that Chauncey had booked, overlooking Central Park.

"It's beautiful, Chauncey, but if I'm not mistaken this is a honeymoon suite."

"Yes it is, but to us it is a pre-honeymoon suite. Champagne and strawberries right here."

Chauncey picked up a strawberry and pulled Max to him, dangling the strawberry so that it just touched his lips. Max pulled the strawberry with his lips into his mouth.

"Lucky little strawberry," Chauncey said, with envy. He kissed Max again, opening his mouth, and licking the strawberry. Then he stopped and poured the champagne. "Yes, that is one lucky strawberry," he said, and licked his lips.

Max already wanted Chauncey. One touch was all it took. The champagne was delicious, and Max downed two glasses. Chauncey set his empty glass on the counter, and licked the champagne off of Max's lips. His hands were helping themselves to Max's pants, pushing them down and grabbing Max's ass. He looked down at Max's hardness and licked his lips again.

"Is that for me?"

"That is always for you," Max said, and playfully touched himself. He was already buzzed from the champagne, and it felt good to let loose, especially with Chauncey. He pulled Max's shirt up and over his head and looked at him.

"Look what I've got tonight," he said, as he admired Max's body. He picked Max up and pulled his legs around him, holding his butt cheeks apart. He began to walk toward the bedroom, passing the windows.

"Chauncey, everyone will see me," Max said, as he looked out the windows.

Chauncey moved even closer to the window. "That's right, baby. Look what's mine, New York City, and all mine," he said proudly, as he backed Max's naked ass up to the window. He fondled Max's naked butt and Max laid his head on his shoulder. Max cherished Chauncey and his unashamed love for him.

"Well, I think New York has seen enough. It's time for you to go to bed."

Chauncey carried Max to the bed and placed him in the middle of it, opening his legs for a good view. "There's my baby," he said, as he quickly took off his clothes. He stood looking at Max for awhile. Chauncey's admiration for his body used to embarrass Max, but now it was a turn-on. The more Chauncey stared, the harder Max got. Max pulled his heavy balls up for display.

"See something you like?"

Chauncey was on the bed now, and removed Max's hand from his balls. "Sure do," he said, and lifted Max's heavy balls with his tongue. "I sure have been neglecting my baby. These are heavier than they were last time. I've got to do better."

Max laughed, and Chauncey moved up and kissed him on the mouth. He massaged Max's head and kissed him deeply. He moved down and kissed Max's neck and chest, sucking at his nipples, nipping at them just enough to cause Max's arousal to grow even more.

"Oh, Chauncey, you spoil me."

"Mm, you know it, baby," Chauncey replied, and kept on kissing and licking and sucking on Max. He opened Max's legs so that he could get in between them. His expert tongue played on Max's balls, squeezing them inside his mouth. He loved Max and it was very evident in the way he made love to him, every time. Chauncey fondled and played with Max's balls with his mouth and his tongue, and Max's body once again went limp, surrendering itself completely to Chauncey's sexual arousing.

"Ohh," he moaned, and Chauncey licked up along Max's shaft and let his tongue find the little slit at the top of the pulsating head. Max put his hands on Chauncey's head and played with his hair.

"Suck me, Chauncey, oh please."

Chauncey took Max's pole of joy into his mouth and deep into his throat. Max had never pleaded with him, and Chauncey was not going to withhold his love from Max, not now, not ever. He massaged Max's inner thighs and stroked him deep beneath his balls as he pulled hard with his mouth on Max's cock. Max was thrusting upward, wanting more and more of

Chauncey, needing his love, begging for his touch. Chauncey stroked, and pulled, caressed and kissed Max until he felt the first burst from Max's very heavy cum filled balls. He slid his fingers between Max's butt cheeks, and entered him, quickly finding that most sensual place deep inside Max. Max continued to shoot burst after burst of the warm yummy sauce that Chauncey craved.

"Ohh," Max moaned louder than usual as he spread his legs wide for his lover, never wanting him to stop. "Don't stop, don't stop," he said, again and again, and Chauncey did not stop. He could bring pleasure to Max all day and all night. Max's balls had finally emptied themselves, but Chauncey did not stop sucking until he felt Max's hard throbbing penis become soft in his mouth, and he had been given every drop of Max's wonderful sauce.

"Fuck me, Chauncey, fuck me hard now," Max demanded.

Chauncey let his sweet little rod of joy slide out of his mouth, and then he lifted Max's legs onto his shoulders and entered Max's ready opening, stroking and squeezing Max's sweet ass with his hands as he thrust hard at Max's commanding.

"That's so good, Chauncey. You're so good. You fuck me good."

Chauncey watched Max's face as he lost himself in Max's love. He held Max's butt with his hands pushing upward as he thrust against Max's zone of most intense pleasure. Chauncey came deep into Max, and Max's very last burst shot from his dick onto his skin.

"How's my baby?" Chauncey asked.

"Ohh, so good," Max moaned in response. They lay beside each other and dozed for a little while.

When they awoke, they decided it was time to check out the rings that would symbolize the never ending love they most definitely felt for each other. It was beautiful outside, so they walked in the park awhile before shopping. They held hands as they walked, and watched the joggers as they passed them by. A young woman jogged up behind them and as she passed, she glanced back, and then slowed to a stop.

"Hi, Mr. Turner, hi, Chauncey," she said.

"Oh, hi, Kate," Max said. "I didn't recognize you with your hair in a ponytail. How are you?"

"I'm fine. I start working for an investment firm on Monday, so I'm taking advantage of the nice weather. What are you two doing in New York?"

"We thought we'd see a play, just get away," Max said, careful not to offer too much.

"You know, I'm really sorry about everything. Um, Nick and I aren't together anymore. He went back to England. I just didn't want to go back. I missed my family in Philly."

"Thank you, Kate. We wish you well, honey."

"You know, I hope that someday Nick will see what the two of you have," she said, smiled, and jogged on.

Max turned to Chauncey and smiled. Then he hugged him. "Maybe he will, Chauncey, maybe he will."

Chauncey held Max for as long Max wanted to be held, and then the two of them continued their walk in the park, hand in hand.

Head Games

When Roman answers an ad to work at ManGrowth Manor, a specialty hospital for men only and a place that Roman has never heard of, he is unclear of his duties at the institution and even more confused about the mission of the hospital itself. After being given a brief tour of ManGrowth Manor, Roman is still uncertain about the job, but he decides to give it a chance. It doesn't take long, however, for Roman to realize that there is something very odd about ManGrowth Manor and he wonders if the expectations of him are quite different than had originally been explained.

Roman was less than thrilled to be working this summer, and he was even less thrilled to be working at a hospital. But he knew that graduate school was important these days, and he also knew that if he didn't get his master's degree now, he probably never would. "Money is money," he grumbled, as he drove to work that first morning.

Roman had never been this far north on the Upper Peninsula of Michigan, and he had never heard of this particular hospital. It was well hidden by massive trees and thick undergrowth. Roman parked his car in the employee lot and walked slowly toward the front entrance. "Man, this place is old," he mumbled. The door made an eerie sound as Roman opened it. He walked down a long hallway until he came to a door that read, "Human Resources," and walked inside.

"Come in, Roman. I'm Gianni. I have some forms for you to fill out, and then we can get you started."

Roman took the forms and sat down at the little table in the corner. He hurriedly filled in the necessary information and then handed the forms to Gianni.

"Very well, Roman. Mr. Osio's office is at the end of the hallway. He will be your supervisor."

Roman nodded, and slowly made his way down the long hallway to Mr. Osio's office.

On his way to Mr. Osio's office, Roman immediately noticed a man in a hospital gown. What is a patient doing here in the administration building? The hospital is behind this building and across the lawn. Roman stared at the man who appeared to be mumbling to himself.

"Hey," the man said.

Roman said "Hey" to the man.

Then the man again said, "Hey, hey, hey."

Roman waved to him, and walked on toward Mr. Osio's office.

"Roman, it's good to meet you. I've heard great things about you, young man." Roman sat down, and Mr. Osio spoke very directly to him. "Roman, you do know the mission of our wonderful facility here, correct?"

Roman thought this a very odd question, and replied, "I guess so."

Mr. Osio had a feeling that Roman did not know the hospital's mission. "This is a facility for men only, Roman, and a facility for a very specific type of men."

Roman was listening, but he still did not know what the man had meant. Was he supposed to know? His graduate advisor hadn't mentioned anything about this being a "special kind" of hospital. Roman tried to remember the name of the hospital, but was having trouble with that. What did the sign say? Roman couldn't remember. He had been too busy trying to drive through the overgrown trees and thick foliage to pay much attention to the sign. "I'm not sure if I understand, sir?"

"We pride ourselves on our mission, Roman. The Upper Peninsula of Michigan was chosen specifically for our very special mission. It's nice up here, don't you think? We have the lakes, and the cooler weather is good for our patients, Roman. It decreases anxiety and tendencies toward anger outbursts."

Roman continued to listen, but he still did not "get" what the man was trying to say.

"Our mission here at ManGrowth Manor is to assist those who come here in becoming the men they were born to be, but have perhaps become a little confused during adolescence or at some other time about their proper role as men in society. We believe that this confusion may have occurred as the result of some traumatic event in the lives of some of these men."

Roman was becoming more and more confused the longer Mr. Osio talked. What the fuck is he trying to say?

"Roman, the men who have come to ManGrowth Manor have not come of their own free will. They are here as the result of a very concerned family member or perhaps a member of the clergy. As a result, the men here at ManGrowth Manor are here by court order."

Roman's eyes opened wide at this last statement. "Are they dangerous?"

Mr. Osio sighed. "They will not physically harm you, Roman, but they do pose a danger to society. They have defied the natural order of man, Roman."

Shit, man, would you just fucking say something in plain English, Roman thought. The man was talking in riddles, or he may as well have been as far as Roman was concerned.

"Roman, do you understand?"

Does the fucked up expression on my face tell you anything, Roman wanted to ask. "I'm not sure," he said. Roman didn't want to seem stupid, but did want to know what he had gotten himself into.

"ManGrowth Manor, Roman, is a facility for men who have expressed feelings for other men the way they should be expressing feelings toward women. Some have openly confessed to these feelings, and others, well, unfortunately, others have actually been discovered with men in the way they should desire to be with women, and that is, in a sexual way. The men here at ManGrowth Manor are confused, Roman, but when they leave here they are prepared to fulfill their natural place in society, as real men."

The emphasis that Mr. Osio had placed on the word "real" disturbed Roman. Did the university know about this? Did they know that such a place as ManGrowth Manor existed today? This was not the 1950s. Shit, the 1950s were over sixty years ago. Time did pass up here in the Upper Peninsula of Michigan just as it did everywhere else, didn't it?

"Roman, do you understand now?"

Roman nodded. What was he supposed to do or say at that question?

"I will take you on a tour of our magnificent facility in a few minutes. The hospital is divided into three wings, Roman. Wing One is for those men who have demonstrated a propensity for the finer things in life, the things a woman enjoys. These are the men who require the shortest amount of time with us, roughly three to six months."

Roman thought that that was a long time. He couldn't imagine what the other floors were reserved for.

Mr. Osio continued. "Wing Two houses men who have expressed a desire to, well, actually be with another man. They usually stay with us for a year or two."

Roman tried not to look stunned, but he was shocked. He was shocked at everything Mr. Osio had said. He was mostly shocked at Mr. Osio's belief in his own crap that he was spewing.

"Now, Roman, for Wing Three. These are the men who are the most difficult to help. The men on Wing Three have been with a man in the way that they were meant to be with a woman. Some have come here actually believing that they have loved another man, and that they still do love a man. It is very difficult to work with these men, Roman, because it appears that they are experiencing a period of mourning. They are depressed. They cry out for their presumed loved one. It is sad to see them like this, but when they finally leave ManGrowth Manor, they are ready to be husbands and fathers. It is very rewarding for us to have helped these men find their way, the right way, the way they should be, and the way they know deep down that they should be."

Roman was in shock. He felt like he had just taken a huge step back in time. Maybe this guy has never left this old place. The building and what I've seen of the grounds so far certainly appear as if they belong in the 1950s or sometime around then or before then, he thought.

Mr. Osio stood up. "Well, let's take a look around, shall we?"

Roman said nothing, but he followed Mr. Osio through the underground hallway that connected the administration building to the main hospital.

Mr. Osio opened the door to Wing One and escorted Roman to the various rooms. The hospital was ugly in Roman's opinion. The walls were plain and depressing. There was a small window at the top of each door. "The window at the top of each door is a 'special' window, Roman. The staff can see in, but the patients do not know that they are being observed. The patients cannot see out through the window. We need to know how the men are spending their time. You do know what masturbation is, don't you, Roman?"

Roman almost choked at Mr. Osio's question, but coughed instead. "Yes, I do," Roman answered.

"We discourage it here, Roman. The men have visitors often, however, assigned visitors, prostitutes mostly. They come to encourage the men to desire women, and of course, to satisfy the men's sexual needs."

Roman wanted to leave. He had seen enough and had heard far too much. If the money wasn't as good as it was here, he would have left before this little tour had begun. But over the summer he would make three times what he would make flipping burgers like his friends were doing. Still, flipping burgers was beginning to look very good to Roman now.

Mr. Osio led Roman to a flight of stairs and up to Wing Two. "Wing Two can be quite intense, Roman. The men have a lot of mental health specialists who visit them, and they visit often. In the minds of these men, they have become confused about who they truly are as men, and discovering what traumatic event caused this confusion can be extremely difficult. Sometimes the cause is not discovered at all, and the men must then be moved up to Wing Three."

Roman followed Mr. Osio up another flight of stairs to Wing Three. "The men here on Wing Three are visited daily by both mental health professionals as well as by our 'ladies', if you will. Some of the men on Wing Three have become so confused, Roman, that they show no interest whatsoever in even the most beautiful of women, neither physical interest nor emotional interest."

Roman almost laughed out loud when Mr. Osio looked directly at his crotch when making the comment about "physical interest."

I get it, Roman thought. The men can't get it up for a woman. Why don't *you* get it, Mr. Osio? Roman was more than a little appalled after his brief tour, but he needed the money for graduate school, so here he was for the summer.

Roman walked with Mr. Osio back to his office. "Your job, Roman, is to talk with the men, listen to them, and try to remember why they are here and what our mission is here at ManGrowth Manor. Well, I have work to do, Roman. Here are the charts for your room assignments. You will pick these up at the front desk every morning."

Mr. Osio stood up and shook Roman's hand. "Welcome to ManGrowth Manor, Roman."

Roman shook the man's hand weakly, and then headed back to the hospital. Mr. Osio was a bit uncomfortable with the lack of strength in Roman's handshake. He picked up his recorder and turned it to record. "Note to self: Roman Joyce, the new orderly, may have 'tendencies'. I will personally keep a close eye on this young man." Mr. Osio turned off his recorder and placed it back into his desk drawer.

Roman tapped lightly on the door of his first patient assignment. Not waiting for a response, Roman opened the door. The man had been writing something in a tablet. "Oh, hi, I'm Roman."

"I'm Steve," the man said.

"Were you writing? I don't mean to interrupt."

"Here," the man said, shoving the tablet at Roman.

Roman looked at the very elaborate drawing on the paper.

"This is extremely good," Roman said.

The man looked at Roman. "What?"

"It's so perfect, every detail is perfect," Roman said.

"Well, you are either lying to me, or you have no idea what the mission of ManGrowth Manor is," the man said, somewhat bitterly and sarcastically.

"I'm not lying, sir. This is beautiful. Every detail of this gown is perfect. It belongs on the Red Carpet for sure."

The man then brought out his other designs and presented them proudly to Roman.

Roman proclaimed every one of the man's designs as beautiful. "I hope you do well with your designs," Roman said to the man.

"Are you crazy? I can't actually *make* these. I was sent here because I *want* to make these, but society says I'm not supposed to want to make these."

The man's words were biting, and Roman felt bad for him. "I, I'm sorry, sir."

The man ignored Roman's apology and went back to his drawing.

Roman left the man's room and walked down the hall. He was supposed to write notes on each man he visited, what the man was doing when he entered the room, and what the man had said during their conversation. If the man was doing nothing extraordinary, Roman was to document, "Pleasant to approach. Nothing to note." That is what Roman documented after he left the man's room. But the man *was* doing something extraordinary, something wonderful. But Roman knew his idea of extraordinary would not be considered as positive here at ManGrowth Manor. Besides, Roman wanted to meet more of these so called "perverts." Mr. Osio had not actually said the word "pervert", but Roman knew that the man had wanted to say it.

Roman was assigned one patient from every floor, so he walked up the steps to the second floor. He knocked on the door, and then walked into the room. "Hi, I'm Roman."

"My name is Rodney," the young man said.

"You were reading?" Roman asked.

Rodney looked down, and then slowly uncovered the book he was reading. "Here," he said, handing it to Roman.

Roman looked at it. "I love this poem. I've read all of this man's works."

Rodney looked at Roman, not believing him. "Oh, really. Well, then, what does the last sentence of 'Two Loves' mean, huh? What does Lord Alfred Douglas mean when he writes, 'I am the love that dare not speak its name'?"

Roman looked at Rodney's sad eyes. "It is the love between two men, Rodney."

Rodney was impressed, but nonetheless distrustful of this new person. "Very good, Einstein. So, do you think you deserve a medal now, an award of some kind?"

Roman looked at Rodney. He felt bad for him, and could definitely understand his bitterness. "No, I don't," Roman said, answering Rodney's question.

"If you don't mind then, I would prefer being alone," Rodney said, and Roman left the room. He wrote the same remarks in Rodney's chart that he had written in the first man's chart. Roman didn't want to do anything that would make these men's sentences any longer than they already were. And yes, Roman considered being here a sentence.

Roman walked slowly to the third floor. He looked at the name on the chart. "Chuck Matthews," it read. The last entry in the man's chart made Roman very curious about him. This Chuck Matthews was Roman's age, and had been in graduate school. "Failed to take an interest in sports. Spoke of lost love affair as an undergraduate. Pursuing graduate degree in literature. Roommate had discovered numerous items related to pulp fiction." This is insane, thought Roman. Who the fuck cares what the man reads? Who runs this place, anyway? Roman looked around to see if anyone was watching, and then he flipped through Chuck Matthews' chart, paying special attention to the back of the chart. He couldn't find anything that indicated who actually ran this place. The only thing Roman could find was "ManGrowth Manor" stamped on every page of the chart in big bold letters. Guess they're proud of that, he said, and knocked on Chuck's door.

There was no answer from inside the room, so Roman walked quietly inside. "Mr. Matthews?" Chuck was curled up on his bed facing away from Roman. "Mr. Matthews?"

"Yes," the man said.

"I'm Roman, a new orderly here."

The man opened his eyes, but continued to stare at the wall. "I'm sorry?" he asked.

Roman repeated what he had just said. Chuck had to be sure before he looked at Roman.

"Roman, it's me, Chase," the man said.

"Chase?" Roman hurried to the man's bed.

"Be careful, Roman. They are watching." Roman stood up and took a couple of steps back.

"There was no one in the hall. I don't think anyone is watching," Roman assured him.

"Roman, you're a fool, and if you don't think you're being watched every single minute of the day that you are inside this living hell, then you are a damned fool."

Roman lowered his voice. "How do you know that, Chase?"

"I just do, okay. And you had better call me Chuck when you're here. That's my new name. They think it's a much more manly name."

"How long have you been here?" Roman asked.

"Long enough, but not as long as most. I'm scheduled to leave soon. I played their game, if you know what I mean."

Roman shrugged his shoulders. He was beginning to at least think he knew what Chase meant. "But why are you here, Chase, and how did it happen?"

Chase glared at Roman. "I think you know the 'why', and the 'how' is because my roommate found my magazines and then he read my letter. If I ever see that fucker, I swear, I will kill him."

"Your roommate?"

"Yeah, Scott. Scott was my roommate and believe me, he loved having my dick in his mouth. He would suck my cock so hard that I would swear it was going to come off in his mouth." Chase grabbed his crotch to emphasize his point. "Damned good head, though."

"But the letter, Chase, what was that about?"

"It was about you, Roman. I missed you. You know how hot and heavy we were, and you know we weren't just fooling around," he said, defiantly.

"I never said we were," Roman defended himself. "God, I've been trying to find you for the last year, Chase. I called everyone I could think of who might have known your whereabouts."

"Well, loverboy, I've been right here."

Roman sat in a chair beside the bed. "Why did he do it, your roommate?"

Chase pulled out the letter that he had kept hidden. "Here, read it," he said. Roman took the letter and read it. It was a love letter to him.

"This is beautiful, Chase. I'm so sorry."

Chase took the letter back and hid it again. "When Scott found it, he became extremely jealous, plain and simple. I was just fooling around with Scott, but he was getting too serious. I didn't love him and I told him so, and so he called this place as a revenge."

"I swear, Chase, I had no idea this place existed. It's as if time has never passed here."

Chase looked at his former lover. "It hasn't, Roman. They make us believe that we're confused or something."

Roman had so many questions for Chase that he didn't know where to begin. "How did your roommate know about this place?"

"I'm not sure, Roman, but he grew up around here and probably just knew. You can't see this place from the road. It's hidden very well, and so are its secrets. But like I said, I'm almost out of here, and I'm going across the border just as soon as I am out of here for sure. It's not far, you know. I overheard a couple of the nurses one day saying that it was less than five miles from here to Canada. One of them has a boyfriend up there."

Roman still could not understand how people got put in this place. "So, one phone call is all it takes?"

"One phone call and one love letter, or acting a little effeminate, or doing something that *they* consider to be effeminate is all it takes to get put in here, but there is definitely something wrong with this place. That Dr. Osio is one nut job, that's for sure."

"Chase, did you say *Dr.* Osio?"

"Yeah, I'm sure you met him. He runs the place."

"I met him, but he introduced himself as *Mr.* Osio, not *Dr.* Osio."

"Oh, believe me, he's a doctor, a doctor of psychiatry, no less. Go figure. He's a real nut job, too. I know he comes up here at night, too. I've caught him looking in my room when he didn't think I was awake. I give him the show he's looking for, too. I pretend to be asleep, and then I start jerking off just enough to get good and hard and then I get naked, spread my legs, and just lie here in all my glory. I know he's out there just dying to take my thick hard cock into his mouth or maybe up his ass, and probably both."

Roman was shocked, but he had known Chase for a long time and knew that he wouldn't make this shit up. "Damn, Chase, does he ever…"

"Does he ever steal a cookie from the cookie jar?" Chase completed Roman's question for him.

Roman laughed a little at Chase's comment. "Yeah, does he?" Roman asked.

"Not *this* cookie jar, he doesn't, but he has tried."

Roman looked at Chase. "That's right, Roman. Dr. Wonderful plays this game, you see. He finds the men who are especially vulnerable and then he tries to console them. He came into my room one night, saw me in the same position that you did, and then he lay down beside me and put his arm around me. Then he got as close to me as he possibly could. He was hard, too, Roman. I could feel his old man hard-on pressing against my ass. He ran his hand along my chest, talking real nice and all, and then I felt his hand inside my shorts." Chase laughed at his own story.

"What's so funny, Chase?"

"I yanked his hand back out of my shorts and looked right at him. I'll never forget the look on his face when I said, 'I don't want you, doctor'. He looked hurt, Roman, and I loved it. The man's a fag, and he has built himself his own little utopia here. Now do you get it?"

Roman looked dazed. "Damn, Chase, the man is an evil genious," he said.

"Tell me about it. He gets his rocks off, all the while convincing his victims that it's all in the name of therapy. Then, when he wants some new meat, he declares somebody rehabilitated or whatever he calls it, and lets them leave his wonderful ManGrowth Manor. That way he makes room for a fresh new cock."

Roman knew that it was getting late and that he should be going, but he wanted to know everything about this place. "But, why did Scott want you to be put in here? Why didn't he just find a new guy?"

Chase whispered, "I think Scott was afraid of being sent here himself. When you grow up here in the Upper Peninsula of

Michigan, you just know about this place. If good old Dr. Osio doesn't want you to leave, you don't leave. If he wants you to stay, if he likes what he's getting from you, then you stay."

Roman looked up at the window in the door. "Can you see out?" he asked quietly.

"Of course we can, but no one tries because they've been brainwashed, but not me. I wait until Dr. Osio makes his 'nightly rounds' and then I watch to see where he goes. I must admit, though, that the good doctor certainly knows how to manipulate minds. Come here, Roman."

Roman followed Chase into the tiny bathroom. He removed a small picture from the wall. "Look through this." He showed Roman a tiny hole that he had made over the past year. "I would hear moans and voices in here, and I just had to find out what was going on. That's Wally's room. The poor fucker is one of Dr. Osio's favorites. But, I have to admit, seeing the old fag with his face covered with cum is better than anything on television."

Roman helped Chase replace the picture. "When you're in here, you can't be seen?" Roman asked.

"Not if you keep the door open. That's another secret." Chase showed Roman how the window in the door to his room reflected through the window in the bathroom door. "See. If you don't close the door, you can't be seen in here. Clever of me, don't you think?"

"Shit, yes, Chase. But, you were always smarter than the teacher." Chase raised his eyebrows, in devilish agreement.

"I'd better go now, Chase. See you tomorrow, okay?"

Chase nodded.

Roman walked out the door and down the hall to return his charts for the day. It was only three in the afternoon, but already Dr. Osio's door was closed and locked. Roman left the charts with the clerk, and drove the hour drive back to civilization. He wouldn't have gone back to the hospital the next day if it weren't for Chase, or Chuck. He still wanted Chase, and now he felt guilty about leaving him when he had.

The following day, Roman had been assigned the same three men as the day before. Steve had drawn more exquisite designs which Roman knew should be made into beautiful gowns and worn to the most elegant of parties, not rotting away on a tablet and kept in this awful place.

Rodney was reading more poetry when Roman stopped by. "Come to impress me with your literary knowledge again?"

Roman had to admit that the guy had some spunk. He didn't apologize for doing what he enjoyed. "No, Rodney. I brought you something."

"Yeah, whatcha got?"

Roman handed Rodney two books that he thought he might like.

"Are you crazy? You can't bring those in here, and I can't get caught with them."

"Suit yourself. I'll just take these back home with me then."

Roman started to put the books away when Rodney stopped him. "No. I'll hide them somewhere," he said, a little sarcastically, but Roman knew that Rodney appreciated what he had done for him.

Roman couldn't wait to see Chase again. He hurried up the back stairs to the third floor. He was surprised to pass Dr. Osio in the hall. "Good to see you again, Roman," he said.

"Dr. Osio," Roman replied. Roman watched as Dr. Osio walked the other way, wondering if he had noticed that Roman had addressed him as doctor today. If he had noticed, he hadn't let it be known to Roman.

Roman waited to knock on Chase's door until Dr. Osio had left the floor. Roman knocked, but there was no answer. Roman cleared his throat and knocked harder. Then he opened the door. "Chase?"

"Shh, in here, Roman, and shut the door."

Roman closed the door and walked into the tiny bathroom.

"Come here, Roman."

Chase was sitting cross-legged in the small bathtub, completely naked. Roman set his stuff down and went to him. Chase motioned to him to sit on the edge of the bathtub. Roman sat on the edge of the tub and looked into Chase's eyes. Chase pulled on Roman's tie, forcing his lips down to his own. Roman kissed Chase the way Chase had remembered.

Roman closed his eyes and let Chase take him to where he had remembered. He missed Chase. "Oh, Chase," he whispered.

Chase pushed Roman back and looked at him, stroking his tie. "Remember how it was between us, Roman? It was hot. It was hotter than hot."

Roman slid into the bathtub onto his knees and grabbed Chase. He pulled Chase's mouth to his, forcing his tongue inside. Chase pulled Roman's shirt up and out of his pants. The feel of Chase's hands on his naked skin made Roman moan. Chase looked at Roman.

"Suck me, Roman. You know you want to."

Roman did want to. The bathtub was so small that Chase had to stand up.

"Lean over me, Chase."

Chase leaned over Roman and Roman ran his warm hands upward along the back of Chase's legs. The swollen head of Chase's cock bobbed tauntingly at Roman's lips. He wrapped his tongue around the swollen head, and Chase leaned all the way over Roman.

"Oh, fuck, Roman."

"Mmm," Roman teased. He slowly took Chase's cock into his mouth, swirling his tongue around it as it entered. Then he held it half in and half out. Chase bent his knees and pushed against Roman, trying to force his cock all the way into Roman's mouth.

"Shit, Roman, don't tease me now," he said.

Roman had loved teasing Chase sexually, and Chase's mind blowing orgasms were the result of Roman's teasing. Roman lifted Chase just enough so that his legs were dangling and he was completely at Roman's mercy.

"Mmm," Roman moaned, as Chase tried desperately to force his entire dick into Roman's mouth. Roman held Chase's ass with both hands, sliding the tips of his fingers slowly between the two halves, stopping to place the tips of a finger from each hand just barely inside Chase's entrance. Roman could feel the heat from Chase's inner folds on his fingertips. Chase held his breath and waited for more. Then he pulled at Roman's shirt until he had rolled it all the way up. He pressed hard against Roman's back, kneading the flesh, desperately trying to force Roman's body to take him completely.

Chase wrapped his legs around Roman, opening his entrance to him. "Mmm," Roman teased.

"Roman, suck my cock. No one can do it like you. Fuck me with your fingers."

Roman knew what he could do for Chase and he knew exactly how to do it. He opened his mouth wide and then forced his two fingers deeply inside Chase's warm ass, bringing Chase's gorgeous cock into the warm wetness of his mouth.

"Oh, that's it, Roman. Do me good."

Roman sucked hard on Chase's cock, and fucked him expertly with his fingers. All Chase could do now was hold on. He pushed Roman's pants down over his butt and helped himself to Roman's ass. Roman had Chase dangling upside down, but neither of them cared. It had always been this way with them, raw, hot sex. Chase had missed Roman's long thick fingers. He was doing him good, stroking him deep, and sucking him hard. Chase moaned, each moan louder than the one before, until he could feel the cum rising from his heavy balls. He reached around Roman's sexy ass and forced his hands inside Roman's pants, not bothering to unzip them. He pulled Roman's cock up and began making full long strokes with his hands. Then he quickened his pace, faster and faster. Roman leaned back, and Chase pulled Roman's balls up, molding them with one hand and pulling Roman's cock forcefully with the other hand.

"Roman, Roman," Chase moaned, and he felt his balls emptying and the cum exploding from the end of his dick. He pressed his face against Roman's back to muffle his moans of pleasure.

The vibration against Roman's back was erotic to Roman in a strange way, and he muffled his own moans with the thick meaty cock in his mouth of the lover he had missed. The vibrations of Roman's muffled moans around his cock caused the very last of Chase's cum to shoot out with a force that made his entire body jerk. Roman continued to suck Chase's cock until it would no longer stay within his mouth's grasp. Chase could feel the heated breath of Roman against his balls as the two men both struggled to steady their breathing.

Roman lifted Chase up and back over him, and held him in his lap. Chase's face had developed a scarlet hue from him hanging head down for so long. Chase closed his eyes.

Roman looked at him. "Chase," he said.

Chase slowly opened his eyes again. "Damn, Roman."

Drained, it took the two former lovers several minutes before they could move.

Roman started to walk out of the bathroom, pulling his pants up as he went. "Roman, no, they'll see you, remember?"

Roman hurried back into the bathroom and put his hand on the door.

"No, leave it open, remember? You can't forget these things, Roman."

Roman dressed in the bathroom, and Chase waited several minutes and then dressed and joined Roman in his room. "That's how we have to do it here?" Roman asked, not needing an answer. Roman looked out through the window at the top of Chase's door. "You really can see out. I can see the entire hallway, both ways."

"I told you, Roman. Most of the men are afraid to look because they have been brainwashed into thinking that they cannot see out."

"No one is out there," Roman said.

"I know. They come around in the morning. You probably saw Dr. Osio on your way up."

Roman nodded that he had.

"He'll be back tonight. I just hope we weren't too loud, you know. I don't want 'the chosen one' in the next room to know about us."

"Why does Wally let him do it, Chase?"

"You should hear him, Roman. Dr. Osio, I mean. He's sick. He has convinced Wally that he needs him and his touch every night in order to get over the love that he has lost, and

Wally is so brainwashed that he has forgotten that that lost love is what got him put into this hell hole to begin with."

They continued to keep their voices low. "Have you ever talked to Wally?" Roman asked.

"Only a couple of times. He's too brainwashed to help, really. It's sad, too, because I think Dr. Osio is about done with him, you know. He's ready for someone new, a fresh cock. So every night I listen for awhile. I think Dr. Osio is trying to convince Wally that he is well and that his 'night sessions' have helped him get through his pain. But it's crap, Roman. Wally is the one who will suffer when he gets out of here. He thinks Dr. Osio really cares about him."

Roman hated this place more and more each day, and what it was doing to guys just like him. He could have very easily been where Chase is now. He felt sick and had to sit down. "What's wrong, Roman?"

"This whole place is wrong, Chase. It's terribly distorted."

"You're telling me, buddy. But what can we do?"

Roman shrugged his shoulders. "I don't know, Chase, but I'll think of something. I promise."

Before Roman left that day, he leaned over Chase on the bed and kissed him. He opened Chase's legs and slid his hand up along Chase's solid butt. "I missed you, Chase. We were good together, weren't we? We were hot."

Chase held Roman's head with his hands and sucked his tongue into his mouth. When he finally let it go, Chase licked his lips. "Wish that was your dick," he said.

Roman felt a tingling in his jeans. "Shit, you're making me hard again, Chase. See you tomorrow, buddy. You hanging in there okay? I promise I'll get you out of here."

Chase nodded that he was doing okay.

Roman left Chase and walked down the stairs to drop off his charts for the day. Dr. Osio was still in his office, with the door open. "Come in for a minute, won't you, Roman?"

"Fuck, almost made it out," he mumbled.

"Yes, Dr. Osio," Roman said, walking seemingly unafraid into the demented doctor's office.

Dr. Osio got up and closed the door. "So, Roman, how are your patients doing?"

Not willing to say anything that might be interpreted as negative, Roman stated, "I'm just an orderly, sir. I'm not qualified to make such assessments."

Dr. Osio looked at Roman, and Roman met his gaze. He's a smart one, this Roman, the doctor said to himself. "But Roman, you are a graduate student. You're very highly educated. Surely you must have some thoughts about their progress. Let's see here. You have seen a young man named Steve, the one who doodles."

Roman wanted to punch this guy out. Steve did not doodle. Steve designed, and Steve's designs were breathtaking. Roman caught himself before speaking. "I believe it's a passing phase, sir. He will do well in the real world. Strikes me as engineer material, don't you think?"

Dr. Osio was determined to catch Roman saying or doing something so that he could force his admission here, too. Dr. Osio had wanted Roman in his bed within minutes of their first meeting. I think young Roman may be on to me, and I certainly can't have that, he thought, as he continued to study Roman's eyes. "And let's see. You have seen Rodney, correct?"

Look at him, pretending not to know which three patients I've been assigned, Roman thought.

"That's correct," Roman answered.

"Any thoughts?" the doctor asked.

Roman thought about Rodney, so defensive, so right, and so well read. "I believe he will do well also."

"And his interest in literature, especially 'that' kind of literature, will pass?"

Roman could feel his jaw clenching and quickly tried to force it to relax. "I believe it will. I am certain that this, too, is simply a passing phase. His current literary interests will wane," Roman assured the doctor.

Hmm, this guy is good, but I do believe that I am just a little better, Dr. Osio was thinking. "That leaves one more patient, does it not?"

Roman was too close to Chase to let Dr. Osio trash him. He tried to stare past Dr. Osio, but the sly doctor moved toward Roman and planted his butt on the edge of his desk so that he was directly in front of Roman.

"Chuck Matthews, yes, you've seen Chuck."

Just hearing Chase's name changed to satisfy the old fart's ego was enough to make Roman snap, almost.

"So, tell me what you think of our Chuck," he said.

"He hasn't much time left here, has he?" asked Roman.

"He was scheduled to leave tomorrow," the doctor said, emphasizing the word "was."

"Then you and your staff have obviously done what was necessary for him," Roman replied, with a smile.

Dr. Osio stood up and walked around the room. "Still, I'm just not sure if he is quite ready to leave ManGrowth Manor. Does he say much about his neighbor, a man named Wally?"

Now Roman was a bit stumped. What was the doctor wanting? "I don't believe that he has mentioned Wally to me," he said.

Then Roman realized that he had almost said Chase's name. Maybe that was what the doctor wanted, for Roman to say Chase and not Chuck.

"And Chuck, is he 'over' his lost love, in your opinion?"

Roman felt his jaw clench and he couldn't stop it from happening. Fuck no, he wanted to say. I'm his lost love, you fuckhead. Roman remained calm, but Dr. Osio did not miss the clenching of his jaw.

"Does he speak of his lost love to you, Roman?"

"No, sir." Roman glanced over his shoulder to see the doctor staring out the window.

"Hmmm," the doctor said. "Well, if he leaves ManGrowth Manor tomorrow, where will he go, Roman?"

"I'm sure that he will follow the discharge orders given by you," Roman said, trying to appease the demented man.

Suddenly changing the subject, Dr. Osio talked more about Wally. "And Chuck never mentioned Wally?"

"No, sir."

"Wally will leave us soon, Roman. Where do you think he should go?"

"As I said, doctor, I know nothing of Wally's history or of his progress," Roman repeated.

The doctor continued to stare out of the window and said, "You may go now, Roman. We will see you tomorrow."

Roman left the charts on the man's desk and hurried out the door, down the long hallway, and out of the building. He drove down the long secluded drive through the thick foliage and away from the dark building as fast as he could.

Roman lay in his bed that night, unable to sleep. He was almost afraid to sleep. He now wished he had a dog or an alarm. He lived alone in his apartment, but in a well lit complex. He could hear his heart beating in his chest. He slept on and off that night until the alarm sounded at six.

Roman didn't have to be at the hospital until nine, but it was an hour's drive. He had thought about not going back, and if it hadn't been for Chase, Roman would not have returned at all. The low paying jobs his buddies had grumbled about doing this summer sounded damned good to Roman right now.

Before Roman left for work that morning, he called his parents back home in Ohio. "Well, Roman, what a nice surprise," his mother said. "How is the job going, honey? Are you learning a lot?"

Roman almost choked. "It's okay," he said.

"Well, you'll be back in school before you know it."

"Yeah. I'm actually looking forward to going back to school, Mom."

"Well, not much is new here, dear. Your father is working some overtime. Summertime is busy at the factory, and I keep busy here at home."

Roman sighed. "Well, I'd better get going, Mom. Good to talk to you."

"Take care, dear," she said.

Roman hung up the phone and sighed. It was good to talk to someone from the real world again. The world he had stumbled into this summer was anything but real.

Roman drove slowly to the hospital, the usual odd feelings beginning to stir as soon as he turned onto the long drive that led through the thick foliage and overgrown trees to the eeriest place he had ever known. The place seemed so desolate, but that was how Dr. Osio kept his dirty little secret hidden from the outside world.

Roman parked his car and walked down the long hallway to pick up his charts. "Good morning, Roman," Dr. Osio said, when they passed each other on Wing One.

Roman said a very quick "good morning" and kept on walking. Roman tapped on Steve's door.

"Well, I guess Dr. Osio thinks I should be an engineer. Said he's got me all set up for an interview at the local technical school. He said you told him that."

"Yes, Steve, I guess I did."

"You and I both know that's not true, so why did you do it?"

"I thought it would help you, you know, to get out of here quickly," Roman replied.

"And into what?" Steve asked.

"You don't have to do it once you get out of here," Roman reminded him.

Steve thought about this. "You're right," he said.

Roman couldn't believe it. Did this quack doctor have this much control over his patient's thoughts? Did he actually convince them that he was in their head for the rest of their lives? Roman looked out of the window at the top of Steve's door.

"You can't see out, you know," Steve reminded Roman.

"Yes, Steve, you can. You've been brainwashed into thinking that you can't."

Steve stood up and walked to the window. He stood on his tiptoes and to his surprise, he could see through the window into the hallway. Then he walked back to his bed.

"I see," he said.

Roman turned around. "Steve, is that all you're going to say?"

"Yes," he said, looking down.

"You've learned to censor absolutely everything you say, haven't you?"

Steve looked at Roman. "You're going to be a good doctor some day, Roman. If you don't mind, I would like to be left alone now."

Roman looked at Steve for a long time, but Steve did not meet his gaze. Roman turned and walked out of the room. He thought about Steve on his way to the second floor. Dr. Osio has really done a number on these guys.

Every day that Roman came here he felt a little more drained when he left. It's as if something, or someone, in this hospital is sucking the life right out of me, he thought.

When he reached the second floor, Roman walked to Rodney's door and looked in through the window before knocking. Rodney was naked. Roman watched as Rodney bent over to pull on his jeans. He wasn't wearing any underwear and Roman watched as the two halves of his butt opened invitingly as he bent over. Roman reached inside his own pants and moved his quickly hardening penis to a more comfortable position. Rodney stood up and Roman watched the gorgeous ass disappear inside its denim prison. Rodney turned around and Roman quickly turned and moved away from the window. Then he remembered what Steve had said. As far as Roman knew, Chase was the only patient here who knew that the window worked from both sides of the door.

Roman looked in through the window of Rodney's room again. He was putting on his shirt and was turned in such a way that Roman could see the big brown nipples on his chest. Roman licked his lips, thinking how he would love to suck those delicious looking little mounds of man flesh. Rodney buttoned his shirt, causing those to disappear, too. Rodney then sat on his bed and picked up a book.

Roman coaxed his own erection back down before he entered the room. "How are you today, Rodney?"

"Okay," he said.

"Guess the doctor thinks I'm going through a phase," he said, a bit sarcastically.

"He knows best," Roman said.

"Is there anything you care to share with me today?"

Rodney looked up and met Roman's stare. "No," he said.

Roman then excused himself and left the room. With the naked picture of Rodney's gorgeous ass fresh in his mind, Roman noted in Rodney's chart that perhaps he wasn't quite ready to be released from ManGrowth Manor.

Roman passed Dr. Osio again when he arrived on Wing Three. "Wally was released this morning," he said to Roman.

"Very good. Is there a new patient?" Roman asked.

"Yes there is, Roman. His name is Bradley. He may need a little extra attention this morning."

"Very well, Dr. Osio," Roman said, and walked on by him and toward Chase's room.

Roman knocked on Chase's door. Then he opened it when there was no answer. Chase was not there. His bed had been slept in, however. Roman went into the bathroom. "Chase?" He must have gone to the cafeteria, or perhaps to the gym.

From the small hole that was hidden behind the picture in Chase's bathroom Roman could hear what sounded like a soft whimpering. Remembering what Dr. Osio had said about Bradley possibly needing extra attention this morning, Roman left Chase's room and tapped lightly on Bradley's door.

"Come in," the voice whimpered.

Roman opened the door to Bradley's room. He looked at the curled up young man on the bed. He looked so young. Roman closed the door to Bradley's room. He walked slowly over to Bradley's bed. Roman felt sorry for the young man who lay staring at the wall. Bradley was shivering. Roman retrieved a heavy blanket from the closet and put it over Bradley. Then Roman removed his own shoes and lay down next to Bradley, holding him in a spooning fashion.

Roman held Bradley closer to him and then joined him underneath the heavy blanket. He whispered softly over Bradley's shoulder, "It's okay, Bradley. I'm here for you."

Bradley began to quiet under Roman's soft comforting voice. Knowing the reason for a patient's admission to Wing Three, Roman said, "Tell me about him, Bradley."

"I loved him, and he loved me," he said.

"Of course you did, Bradley. You miss the sex, don't you?"

Roman ran his hand downward along Bradley's chest and then reached inside his jeans. "Let me help you with your loss, Bradley," Roman said lovingly.

Bradley moved his hands aside so that Roman could unzip his jeans.

"You have a nice cock, Bradley," he said, stroking it to hardness.

The trusting young Bradley slowly rolled onto his back and looked at Roman's loving face. Roman continued to look into Bradley's trusting eyes as he slid the heavy blanket down and slowly removed Bradley's jeans and underwear, completely exposing his fully erect cock.

"You are very beautiful, Bradley," Roman told the young man.

Bradley watched Roman, and Roman let his eyes leave Bradley's eyes for only a second and then his eyes were back on Bradley's very trusting ones.

"May I?" Roman asked, pausing before he took Bradley's perfectly formed cock into his hands.

Bradley nodded, and Roman wrapped his hands around Bradley's cock and slid them slowly upward to the head, where a drop of pre-cum was waiting for him. Bradley opened his legs to Roman's loving touch.

"That's nice, Bradley. That's healthy."

Roman's words were reassuring, and Bradley began to relax.

Roman looked at Bradley's half closed eyes and smiled to himself. Roman lowered his face to Bradley's cock and opened his mouth over the head. His hot breath caused a gasp to escape Bradley's lips. "Mmm," Roman moaned, putting Bradley at ease. Roman held Bradley's young meaty cock in his hand and slowly licked around the head. Then he opened his mouth to

Bradley's young head, holding it between his lips, sucking it tenderly, and then more forcefully as Bradley began to raise his sweet young ass upward. Roman slid his hands between Bradley's legs, stroking him underneath his balls, and kneading the two young globes with his hands as he enjoyed the young cock that was quickly filling his mouth and more. Roman moved his hands between Bradley's half moons, sliding the tips of his fingers along the ribbed crease, stopping to press a finger against Bradley's young hole.

Roman wondered if Bradley was a virgin, and for a moment he thought about how good it would feel to have his own cock deep inside Bradley's young ass. Roman looked up at Bradley's closed eyes. He slid his mouth up and down along Bradley's cock and then stopped for a minute and held the spongy head between his lips.

Roman closed his eyes. In his mind it was his own cock that was being treated so well, as the soft young lips of this gorgeous young man sucked him with just the right amount of pressure. He moaned as he pictured himself naked and being taken completely by this young man. He was opening himself fully to Bradley, and the young man's fingers were stroking him fully and deeply. Roman moaned louder as the young man stroked deeper, and his sucking became more demanding and more forceful.

"Are you ready for the real thing, Roman?"

"Always," he answered.

The young perfect cock entered Roman and made long and deep strokes inside him. Roman was getting close. He grabbed his own cock and held it in his hands.

"You know how hot that makes me, Roman, watching you stroke yourself."

Roman stroked himself for his lover. Roman's lover wrapped his arms around Roman's legs and thrust into him harder and deeper. Roman moaned, and the first burst of cum landed on his chest.

"That's it, Roman. Give me a good show."

Roman gave his lover what he wanted. He moaned and forced even longer and more forceful streams from his cock.

"Oh, shit, Roman," his lover said, and he held tightly to Roman's thighs as he filled him with his warm young cum.

Roman and his lover moaned and screamed each other's names as their climaxes came full and hard.

"Oh, that was good, Roman."

Roman moaned in agreement. "Come here," Roman coaxed, and put his arms out for his lover.

The room was silent. "Come here, you gorgeous sex machine," Roman repeated. Roman felt the body of his lover on his own.

Roman began to speak, but was hushed by his lover's kiss.

"Mmm, you can wake me like this any day, you sexy thing," Roman's lover said.

Roman opened his eyes. His lover kissed his neck. Roman rolled his lover onto his back and sat up. He looked around the room frantically.

"What is it, Roman?"

Roman could hear the rapid beating of his own heart.

"Roman, you okay?"

Roman looked at his lover who was staring at him. A buzzing noise caused Roman to nearly jump off of the bed. "What's that?"

The sound stopped. "It's the alarm. We hear it every morning, Roman."

Roman closed his eyes and then opened them again. He lay back down and put his hand on his forehead.

"I'm going to get into the shower now, Roman. You sure you're okay?"

Roman looked at the man's face. "Yeah, I'm going to rest awhile," Roman assured him. Roman watched as his lover walked to the shower. "Uh, Mike?"

Mike turned around. "I start work at Bob's Burgers today, right?"

"That's your summer dream job," Mike said, with a laugh.

"I get to freeze in the ice cream shop, and you get to fill your lungs with grease fumes this summer. It's the price we pay for choosing graduate school, my friend." Mike walked into the shower. Roman continued to rest. It was a dream. The whole fucking thing was a dream.

Roman got out of bed and joined his lover of several years in the shower. He kissed him passionately, and then looked at him. "We need to make love a lot more often," he said. Before Mike could say a word, Roman's mouth was once again on his.

If You Just Smile

Matt has everything he has ever wanted, or at least he thinks he does. His career is blossoming, and he has recently been promoted to vice president of the bank in the small town where he has worked since graduating from college. Matt's boss is the best, and Matt has lived with his partner and lover, Kent, for the past few years. If there is one thing that Matt would love to change in his life it is the anger which he seems to cause in his lover, yet he has no idea what he is doing to anger him. He does his best to be a good partner to Kent, but he is embarrassed about the black eyes and bruises which he finds very difficult to hide or find excuses for. Matt feels certain that his and Kent's relationship is no different from any other couple's, but when Matt's boss asks him to take his place at a yearly conference, Matt meets a man who shows him an entirely different life from the one that has now become perhaps a little too familiar to him.

Matt awoke in anticipation of the alarm and forced himself to sit up. He sat on the side of the bed trying to force his tired body to come to life. Before getting out of bed, he turned and looked at the man sleeping on the opposite side of the bed. Matt had loved Kent for two years now, and he was certain that Kent loved him. Matt yawned and put his feet on the floor. He stood up and walked slowly to the bathroom, remembering to close the door behind him before turning on the light. Kent worked late and did not want to be awakened at six in the morning.

Matt splashed water on his face and winced when he made the mistake of touching the bruise that he knew was there even before he looked in the mirror. He slowly raised his head until he saw his reflection in the mirror. How the fuck am I going to cover this one up? he wondered. Under his breath, he said, "I'm sure no other men at the bank wear women's makeup."

Matt was a vice president of a bank in his small home town where everyone knew everyone. He and Kent lived about thirty kilometers or so to the south of the small town where Matt had grown up. Matt had met Kent in college and the two had fallen in love within a few short months. Kent had completed only two years of college, stating that it was clearly a waste of time and that he could make more money without a degree in tips alone from bartending.

Matt showered quickly this morning. He knew that it would take a lot of time to cover up the shiner he had gotten last night, and the drive to work seemed to grow longer and longer every day. Matt's days were long and the attention to detail required of a vice president of a bank made him exhausted by the time he arrived home at night. He didn't dare go to bed until Kent came home from work, though, which was often after two in the morning. Kent expected Matt to be available to him every night, and if Matt were asleep when he came home, he would accuse him of being inappreciative of him or thinking that he was better than him because he was the one with the college degree. On more than one occasion, Kent had accused Matt of cheating on him and was certain that that had been the reason Matt had fallen asleep before he had come home.

Matt left the house very quietly and didn't look at the bruise on his face again until he was halfway to work. He felt bad for Kent. Kent had watched as Matt had earned promotion after promotion and was now very well respected in his chosen career and earning a six figure salary, while Kent was still bartending at the same bar and grill where he had worked for six years. Matt looked at his face in the rearview mirror. He tried to dab some makeup on the bruise to cover it up, but this one was determined to be seen. He stopped at the park on the outskirts of town and did his best to cover up the bruise that was already beginning to change colors. It looked darker than it had when he had first seen it that morning. "Maybe no one will notice," he lied to himself.

Matt had already used every excuse he could think of when he had come to work with a bruise. He had no idea how he was going to explain *this* one. He had known women who had been in abusive relationships, but this was much different. Matt was the one with the abusive man, though he was sure that everyone at the bank had assumed that he was married to a woman and that she was the one putting the bruises on his face. It was difficult enough for a man to admit that he had an abusive wife, but if anyone were to discover that Matt's bruises were from another man, a man who was his live-in lover, there was no telling what they would say or do. He might lose his job. And Matt certainly did not want his fellow bankers to know that he was gay. Being gay was tough enough in the larger cities, but in small town America where everyone knew everyone's business, being gay was a different matter entirely.

"Good morning, Matt."

"Good morning, Linda," Matt said, smiling instantly. He hurried to his office, hoping that his sweet motherly secretary hadn't seen the bruise on his face. Matt was early today, as he always was, and began to work on the financial reports that were due in less than a week. He had rearranged his office about a month ago so that he could face away from the door and away from the watchful eyes of everyone who came into the bank, and today he was especially glad that he had done that. When he looked at his reflection in the computer monitor, he was shocked. It appeared as if his face might be swollen a little on the side with the bruise. "Shit," he said, under his breath.

Matt kept as busy as he could for most of the morning, not wanting to talk to anyone today.

"Knock, knock," Linda said. "These are for you, Matt."

Matt made a half turn in his chair. "Thanks, Linda."

The sweet woman left Matt's office, and once he was certain that she had gone, he turned and looked at the beautiful flowers that had been delivered to him. He opened the card, though he knew who they were from. "I love you. You are my life." They were signed, "Love, Kent."

Matt knew that the words on the card were true. Kent just feels bad about himself and about his work situation, Matt had told himself often. He knew that Kent felt trapped in a dead-end job and that Kent's father had been an abusive alcoholic. Kent had told Matt that he had gotten his bad temper from his father. "I can't help it, Matt. That's just the way that I am. It's in my genes."

"He just needs to know that I love him," Matt said, trying to convince himself. The flowers made his office smell good and the aroma was somewhat therapeutic.

Toward the end of the day, the bank president stopped by Matt's office. "Nice flowers, Matt."

"Thanks, John."

"Whoa, were you in a fight there, Matt?"

"No, I, uh, I think I'm still getting the hang of the many dangers that lurk on the farm. It's been awhile since I did much manual labor." Matt thought that sounded at least somewhat believable.

"Well, anyway, that's none of my business, Matt, and that's not what I came to talk to you about. The annual banking conference is next week and I'm in a bind this year."

Matt was concerned for the boss that had been so good to him. "What's up, John?"

"Well, I hate to miss it, Matt. I don't like to push my responsibilities onto others, either. It's Jan. Her due date isn't for another month, but at her doctor's visit today she was discovered to have pre-eclampsia. I guess that's a fancy word for high blood pressure during pregnancy. She needs to have a C-section, Matt."

"Oh, I'm sorry, John. They do expect a good outcome, don't they?"

"Oh, sure. They say the kid is about six and a half pounds already. It's just that I need someone to fill in for me at the conference. You're the best I've got here, Matt. Do you mind going in my place?"

Matt smiled at the somewhat pleading look on his boss' face. "You know I will go, John."

"You're a lifesaver, Matt. I will have everything ready for you, all the reports and whatnot, I promise. It's not all work at these conferences, either. There is plenty of downtime. You'll have fun. And this year the conference is in Denver. You ski?"

"No, I've never tried it."

"Well, once you try it, you will love it. Everything is paid for, so don't worry about going broke."

Matt smiled at his boss. He envied him a little. His wife, Jan, was a real peach. Matt had no use for a wife. He just wished that he didn't make Kent so angry so often. *I just need to be more understanding about Kent's work situation, that's all. I just need to be a better partner to him,* he told himself.

On the drive home that night, Matt felt good about himself. His boss had trusted him to take his place at the most important conference of the year. When he walked into the house, he felt his heart in his throat. *What am I going to tell Kent? This is going to kill him.* Matt decided that he didn't need to say anything to Kent just yet. *I can wait until the weekend to talk to him about the conference. I don't leave until Sunday.* Matt walked into the quaint yet comfortable home that he shared with Kent and set his things down. He walked into the bedroom and then on into the bathroom. "Oh, my God!" he said to the bruised face in the mirror. "John had to have seen this today, not to mention everyone who had walked past the door to my office." He gently touched his face and winced. He very carefully wiped off the makeup, which hid very little, and then he went into the den and poured himself a drink. He watched the news and dozed off and on for a few hours.

He and Kent had had quite a fight the night before. Business hadn't been that good at the bar where Kent worked, and there was talk that his hours might be cut by one day a week. Matt had assured him that he was making enough money for both of them, which had been a hard blow to Kent's pride. "I don't need your pity, Matt," he had said. "I didn't mean it like that, Kent. I just meant that you don't have to worry about money, that's all." Matt played the conversation of the night before over and over in his mind. When Matt had suggested that Kent go back to college and finish his degree, it had been the ultimate blow to Kent's bruised ego, which had ultimately caused the bruise on Matt's face. "You think I'm a fucking failure, is that it?" "No. I didn't mean that at all, Kent." Kent had shoved Matt hard against the wall and struck his face. Matt had thought that he had passed out for a few seconds after that because when he looked up Kent was gone. He had stepped outside to cool off a little. "I just need to be more sensitive. I guess I was pretty thoughtless last night," Matt said to the bruised face in the mirror. It was a little after midnight when Kent walked in. "Matt?"

"In here, Kent."

Kent walked into the den and kissed Matt on the lips. "I love you, baby. Oh, no. I'm so sorry." He held Matt's bruised face in his hands. "You know I don't mean to do it," he said.

"I know you don't, Kent. The flowers were beautiful."

Kent smiled and left the room. Matt heard the shower and he knew that Kent expected him to join him. Matt was tired and needed to sleep, but he would avoid another scene like last night's at almost any cost. Kent opened the door of the shower and pulled Matt inside. "I love you, Matt," he said, and kissed his neck. He kissed Matt's chest and caught the droplets of water that landed on his nipples.

Kent was a damned good lover, and Matt was aroused by his slightest touch. Kent kissed his way down Matt's flat stomach until he reached Matt's cock. Matt's entire body responded to Kent's touch and to Kent's lips, and he moaned. Kent held the top of Matt's cock between his lips and held Matt's balls in his hand. He seductively slid Matt's shower wetted cock into his mouth and looked up at him. Matt looked at Kent and then closed his eyes. His body shuddered. "Oh, Kent," he moaned. Kent opened Matt's legs and held the cute little butt that had been the first thing he had noticed about Matt when they had met. Matt thrust his hard cock into his lover's mouth, and Kent made love to it and to Matt. Matt grabbed onto Kent as his climax began to build and as his climax came full force. Kent continued making love to Matt's cock until Matt was completely drained. "Oh, Kent, I love you so much." "Mmm," Kent moaned in response. Kent wrapped his arms around Matt and looked up at him.

Kent then took Matt by the hand and led him to the bed that the two of them shared. "You always satisfy me, Matt," Kent said, as Matt got onto the bed, preparing to satisfy his lover. Kent entered Matt hard, and Matt tried not to wince. Kent was well endowed and Matt much preferred oral sex, but he could never deny Kent sex. That was just not something that he would do to the man that he loved. "Oh, baby, I love this little butt of yours. You swallow me whole, baby." Kent thrust hard into Matt, and Matt could feel his face begin to hurt as Kent pulled and pushed his body for his own satisfaction. Matt was relieved when Kent finally came. He pulled out, and Matt rolled over onto his back. Kent held him and was soon asleep.

Matt looked at the bedside clock. It was almost two in the morning and he would be up again in just four hours.

Matt awoke just before the alarm and reached over quickly to stop it from buzzing. He quietly got ready for work, leaving early again to try and cover his bruise as best he could, though he was certain that everyone had noticed it yesterday. When he walked into the bank at a little before eight, his boss was already in his office.

"Oh, Matt, thank goodness." John seemed frantic.

"What is it, John?"

"Jan had a very bad night last night, and we are having the baby in two hours. I just stopped in long enough to get things lined out for you. You're the president, Matt, at least for a few days. I should be back in here while you are in Denver."

"Sure, John. Let me know how things turn out. Jan isn't alone right now, is she?"

"Oh, goodness, no. We have all kinds of family around here. The folks at the hospital will no doubt ask half of us to leave. Small towns, you know."

Matt set his things down and moved into John's office temporarily.

"You look good behind my desk, Matt. I'm not sure I like that. Should I be worried?"

Matt knew that his boss was teasing. "I don't think so, John."

John walked through the lobby of the bank on his way out, opening the door for Matt's secretary. "I'm having a baby today," he said happily.

"Well, good for you," Linda told him as he left. She walked to the office where Matt was seated behind John's desk. "I will definitely be updating every one of my e-mail contacts tonight. I am now officially the secretary to the president," she said, proudly.

"Yes, you are," Matt agreed.

"What can I get for you, kind sir?"

Matt laughed at Linda's fake curtsy.

"I'm fine, Linda, but if you are making coffee for yourself…"

"It will be nice and strong," she promised. Linda had a dream job and she knew it. Working for John and Matt made her job not seem like work at all. A woman in her mid fifties, she was a little concerned about Matt's frequent bruises. Like the others, however, she did not think that it was her place to pry into her boss' private life. No one had seen Matt with a woman, but many assumed that he was living with one. He wore no wedding ring, so it was also assumed that he was single. Matt was all business at the bank, and everyone respected that.

Matt looked at John's calendar. Oh, crap, he thought. John was scheduled to work Saturday morning. It was Friday, and Matt was exhausted. He didn't know how he was going to get through today, much less tomorrow morning.

Linda brought his coffee to him and also his airline ticket. "Isn't John something? He put you in first class. Guilt is a wonderful thing sometimes," she said.

"Are you serious? I've never flown first class."

"Well, it's only about an hour and a half flight from here, so don't get too excited. You will need to drive to Kansas City, and your flight leaves Sunday at three in the afternoon."

Matt thanked his nice secretary, and then thought it all through. I have to work tomorrow and Kent works Saturday night, so Sunday morning will be our only time together. Kent hates being alone. He is not going to be happy about me being gone on Sunday. Matt held his head, but touching his face hurt, so he leaned back in John's comfy chair. He couldn't think about that now. He had work to do. He just wished that Kent understood the demands of his job.

Kent surprised Matt that night with the promise of a Saturday morning breakfast. They were both exhausted and went to sleep very soon after Kent came home. Matt was glad that Kent wasn't upset about him working Saturday, but he still hadn't told him about his trip to Denver. It was one thing at a time with Kent. The memory of their last fight was still too fresh in Matt's mind and still too fresh on his cheek to risk angering Kent again. He planned to talk to him at breakfast in the morning.

Kent was an excellent chef, and Matt awoke on Saturday morning to the aroma of a country breakfast. "Mmm, pancakes," he said, as he walked into the kitchen. Kent had gone all out for Matt, and was wearing a chef's apron to top it all off. "Good morning," Kent said cheerily, adding a kiss as Matt sat down to devour the mouthwatering breakfast. "Tomorrow is Sunday, Matt. How about we get away for the day, just the two of us, maybe go to Kansas City. You have Monday off, don't you, since you work today?"

Matt looked down at his plate. "I can't," he said, quietly.

"Why can't you?"

"Kent, my boss is out because his wife had a baby."

"I know. That's why you are working today. But you don't work tomorrow, do you?"

Matt looked up at Kent. "John was scheduled to go to a banking conference next week," he said slowly and calmly, but he could see the hurt in Kent's eyes quickly change to anger.

"You are going to the conference in his place?"

"I have to go, Kent. It's my job."

Kent stood up. "Oh, yes, your hotshot job. You're the big time business man here, aren't you, with your fancy degree in finance. You aren't the loser who quit college, are you?"

"I've never thought of myself as a hotshot, Kent."

"Bullshit." Kent swiped his arm across the kitchen table, crashing the dishes against the wall and onto the floor. "I'm not cleaning that up. You're the hotshot. You can just take off your fancy tie and jacket and do some real work."

Kent left the house, and Matt heard the gravel and rocks hit the side of the house as Kent's old car spun out of the driveway. Matt had no idea where he was going at this early hour on a Saturday, but he couldn't think of that now. He didn't have time to clean up Kent's mess, either. He looked at the syrup that was dripping off of the side of the table and reluctantly began to clean it up. He knew that if he didn't clean it up now, he would be scraping it up later. Matt did what he could, throwing away the broken dishes, and then he left for work.

Matt had forgotten to cover up his bruise this morning, but it hadn't done much good anyway. Linda was the only one at the bank when he walked in. "I had flowers sent to Jan and John," she said. "They have another daughter, Matt. Everyone is fine. I wouldn't be surprised if John came by this morning. He's so proud."

"That's nice, Linda. Thank you." Matt retreated to his office, and Linda was working as a teller today. There were only two other employees in the bank that morning, and Matt hoped that it would be a quiet day. He had no idea where Kent had gone that morning or if he would be there when he got home around one. Matt knew that Kent had to be at work at four this afternoon, but that was all that he knew today. Before Matt left town for the day, he went to the hospital to see his boss and his wife.

"Matt, come on in here and meet Lilly," Jan said proudly.

"Another child named after a flower. Will she ever stop?" John was beaming as he held his baby daughter. Fortunately for Matt, Linda had been kind enough to buy a gift for Matt to give to his boss.

"You will love the conference, Matt. John usually takes me with him. We call it our anniversary because it's the only time of the year when we can get away without the kids. But you will have lots of free time. Who knows, you might meet someone special."

John looked at his wife and smiled, and then looked back at Matt. "She just can't stand to see someone unmarried, Matt."

Matt smiled. The closeness between John and his wife was envied by him. But then, who knows what goes on at home?

"Call me anytime, Matt. If you get into a bind out there in Denver, let me know."

Matt thanked his boss, and then he drove home, not knowing what he would find waiting for him there. It was almost as if Kent were two different people in one body. He could be very thoughtful and lavish Matt with mouthwatering dishes and beautiful flowers, and he always satisfied him sexually. But then, there was a very different Kent, what Matt liked to think of as the anti-Kent. When Kent felt bad about himself, which was more and more often lately, he somehow thought that others were secretly laughing at him or were happy to see him fail. Matt wanted nothing but the best for him. "I just need to try harder to please him," Matt said, as he turned into the drive.

Kent was back. His car was there. Matt felt uneasy, but did not know why. He walked into the house and Kent seemed calm. "Oh, Matt, you're home." Kent walked over to him and kissed him. "Come here. I have something to show you." Kent took Matt by the hand and led him into the kitchen.

"Kent, it's beautiful."

"I bought everything this morning. Now everything is color coordinated." Kent had bought the cutest café curtains in mint green and bright yellow, and had matching dinnerware and candles in the shape of cupcakes. "Do you like it, Matt?"

"I love it, Kent." It did brighten the room that was rather small and bland. Matt really wasn't hungry, but Kent had made lunch for them. "You know, I think I will freshen up the walls with a new coat of paint next week while you're gone. It's time, don't you think?"

"That would be great, Kent."

Kent left for work around three that afternoon, and Matt finally exhaled. He never knew how Kent was going to be at any given time, or which Kent was going to walk through the door, but Kent seemed fine, for now.

Matt pulled out the suitcases and began packing for his week away. He had everything ready to go and had gotten plenty of cash, though his boss had rewarded him with a very generous expense account. He then relaxed and watched some late night television. He was asleep when Kent came home a little after one in the morning. "Hey, sleepyhead," he said, as he nudged him.

"Oh, I'm glad you're home," Matt said, standing up.

"I can see that," Kent said, sarcastically, as he looked at the suitcases packed and ready to go. "It looks like you've been busy," he added, with even more sarcasm.

Matt said nothing. He didn't want to show up at a banking conference bruised any more than he was already. The last bruise was just now beginning to fade.

Kent walked away and began doing something in the kitchen, but Matt did not go and see what he was doing. Matt waited. After awhile, he heard Kent in the bedroom. Matt still waited. He would sleep in the chair if he had to in order to avoid an unnecessary confrontation. Kent walked back into the den where Matt was sitting. "Coming to bed?" he asked, demandingly.

"I'm on my way," Matt said, cheerfully. Matt was surprised when Kent didn't approach him for sex. Matt was tired, but it wasn't like Kent to not want sex. Matt fell asleep with his back to Kent's, feeling unloved and unwanted.

Matt had set the alarm for nine, but he awoke at eight. Kent was sleeping soundly. Matt knew that he had to be on the road soon if he were going to make his flight on time. He had a two hour drive ahead of him and needed to allow at least an hour to check his luggage and make it through security and everything else that was now required before boarding his plane. He waited until ten, hoping that Kent would wake up before he left. He felt bad about leaving him, and he wanted to leave knowing that Kent would be okay without him. He walked into the bedroom and Kent was still sleeping. He knew how much Kent hated to be woken up, so he left him a note. Matt wrote that he would call him and that he loved him. Then he picked up his suitcases and was on his way.

Despite everything that was going on at home, Matt was looking forward to this trip. He had never been to the yearly banking conference and he was eager to listen to the lectures of the leading economists, not to mention the chairman of the Federal Reserve. He had always enjoyed the stimulation of the classroom and missed the idea exchange with his fellow financiers. Matt had arrived at the airport with plenty of time to spare. He bought the latest copy of *The Economist* and waited for his plane. First class was the best and he had more than enough room to stretch his long legs. He had just enough time for a drink during this luxurious flight that went by much too quickly.

The plane landed in Denver and Matt gave the taxi driver the address of the hotel. "Your boss certainly spared no expense, sir. You are staying in one of Denver's finest, with the conference rooms right off of the main lobby." Matt wasn't surprised at John's choice. He probably wouldn't have gone all out for himself, but he had always treated Matt like a son and had taught him everything he knew about the banking industry. Matt's luggage was brought up to his room for him, and John had reserved a suite for Matt, not a room. He opened the door and tipped the man who had brought his luggage. "Enjoy your stay, sir," he said, and left Matt to himself.

Matt looked around the big room. It was spacious, yet cozy. A small kitchenette greeted Matt as he walked inside, with a small living area attached which featured a breathtaking view of the mountains. He walked into the bedroom with attached bath. Proudly advertising its wireless internet throughout, the hotel maintained its old fashioned charm while keeping up with the very latest technology. Matt opened the basket of complimentary snacks and popped one of the small bags of popcorn in the microwave. The aroma of the corn popping reminded him that he hadn't eaten at all that day and the popcorn tasted better than usual. He couldn't wait to tell Kent all about his flight, but no one had answered when he called home. "He must be outside," Matt said, and pulled out the itinerary for the conference. There was a "meet and greet" that night in the main conference room which sounded somewhat interesting to Matt, though he was somewhat shy. "Well, I guess I should go," he said. He showered and put on something casual.

Matt walked into the main conference room and was immediately welcomed by an older gentleman who noticed his name tag.

"I've known John forever. Where is the old man this year?"

"He is celebrating the birth of his third daughter," Matt informed the man.

"Well, good for him. Guess he just won't give up on trying to have a son."

Matt laughed with this nice friend of John. "I don't know about that, but he is definitely outnumbered by the women in his life," Matt added.

"I'm Quinn Dexter. You tell John I said congrats."

"I'll do that," Matt said, and the older man went off to join what Matt had assumed to be a group of more mature bankers. Matt walked over to the bar and ordered a drink.

"You look as lost as I'm sure I do," a man said to Matt.

Matt turned to see a man about his age with a bright smile and bright eyes.

"This is my first conference. Have you been to many?"

Matt admitted that he had not. "My boss usually comes to these, but he and his wife just had a baby," Matt said.

"How nice. Well, I guess that makes us both virgins," the man said.

Matt felt his cheeks immediately begin to get hot.

"I'm Dustin," the man said and held out his hand.

"Matt," Matt said, and shook Dustin's hand.

"Did you fly in, or drive in, Matt?"

"I flew. I'm just one state over, though."

"Well, I was born and raised right here in Denver. If you like to ski, I know the best slopes."

"I've never skied, but I wouldn't mind trying it."

"I'm your man," Dustin said. "We'll go tomorrow. We have the afternoons free this week. They always hold the lectures in the mornings, but never before nine. These conferences are the best kept secret in the industry. This week is like a mini vacation, or so I've been told."

Matt didn't quite know what to say to this very nice and very outgoing man. Matt liked him, though. He seemed nice. Dustin was the president of a bank three times the size of the one that Matt was vice president of, although in Denver Dustin's bank was considered a small bank. Dustin knew almost everyone at the conference, having been in high level meetings with many of them, and he took the time to introduce many of the men and women to Matt. "I have a wonderful vice president, Matt. He stepped down from being president, but he has taught me much more than I ever learned in school. He also outlined the conference for me down to the very hour." Matt smiled at Dustin. "Well, Matt, I will see you tomorrow, bright and early," Dustin said, as he left Matt in the lobby of the hotel.

"Thanks for introducing me to everyone."

"Oh, think nothing of it," Dustin remarked.

Matt took the elevator up to his suite and looked out at the mountains in the distance. He thought about the men and women he had met tonight and wondered what their personal lives were like. He wondered how many of them hid a part of themselves in secrecy or behind makeup. He touched his cheek and hoped that he hadn't looked too odd tonight. The bruise was fading, but he wished that it was gone entirely. It was late and Matt didn't want to disturb Kent, so he went on to bed.

When the phone rang the next morning, Matt picked it up quickly, thinking that it was Kent.

"Good morning. This is your wakeup call," the lady from the lobby greeted.

"Thank you," Matt said, and hung up the phone. It was eight. "I can't believe I slept so long." He felt rested, too. "Must be the thinner air up here," he said. He thought about calling Kent, but it was only seven in the morning back home and he knew that Kent wouldn't be up yet. Kent kept his schedule the same, working or not.

When Matt entered the lobby of the hotel, Dustin was waiting for him. "Here we are again. How was your first night in the Mile High City?"

"It was good. Thanks."

Dustin was his usual upbeat chatty self, just as he had been last night. "Come on. Let's get some breakfast. That's one thing I should warn you about these conferences. You might put on a few pounds. That's what I'm told, anyway." Dustin continued to talk, and he didn't seem to mind if Matt didn't respond right away. He seems so sure of himself, Matt thought. "Well, are you up for your first ski lesson this afternoon?" Dustin was serious. Matt had thought that he was just being polite to the newcomer when he had made the offer to him last night.

"Sure," Matt said.

"Great. You can come with me to my house after the meetings this morning. I'll need to pick up my skis."

"Okay," Matt said, and they settled in for the morning's session. The conferences went from nine until noon every day and the morning flew by. Matt walked with Dustin to his car after the conference.

"You looked as though you were enjoying the lectures, Matt."

"I guess it reminds me of college. I miss it somewhat."

"Hmm, well, did you ever consider going back for a graduate degree? Don't tell me you think you're too old."

"No, I don't think I'm too old, but I don't think it's possible right now," Matt admitted, thinking of Kent.

"I'm not one to lecture, Matt, but I can tell you that a graduate degree opens many doors for you. I finished my Master of Business Administration degree just last summer. I turned twenty-eight last spring and with thirty just around the corner, I thought about what I might do if I woke up one morning and couldn't bear the thought of going to work at the bank. An M.B.A. is a very marketable degree, or at least it looks good on the old resume." Dustin laughed at his own joke, and Matt couldn't help but smile. He also now knew Dustin's age. Matt was twenty-six, and he wouldn't mind going to graduate school, but Kent would never agree to it. He absentmindedly touched his cheek when he thought of Kent. "Well, here we are," Dustin announced, pulling up in front of his house.

It was beautiful. They walked inside, and Matt liked what he saw. "This is nice, Dustin. Did you decorate it?"

"Well, I would hardly call it decorating, but yes, I did. Let me show you around." Dustin showed Matt his home, and Matt saw no signs that a woman was a part of Dustin's life. "I have just what you need for the slopes." Dustin laid everything out for Matt and then changed in another room. "We look like twins," Dustin joked, when he saw Matt again.

The two "twins" arrived at the slopes at around one, and Matt spent more time on his butt than he did on his feet, but he didn't mind. He loved the mountain air, and Dustin was a wonderful teacher. He didn't expect perfection from Matt. He didn't really expect anything from him. All that Dustin seemed to want from Matt was his company. "Well, that's probably enough for today, Matt. You may be sore tomorrow." Matt was having fun and didn't really want it to end, but he knew that Dustin was right. They went back to Dustin's house to change their clothes, and Dustin offered to take Matt out to dinner. "I limit my red meat eating to once a week, but I make that once a week treat really count. How about it, Matt? My favorite steak restaurant, my treat."

"Thank you," Matt said, not knowing what else to say.

They did have a nice time together and Matt found Dustin's conversation stimulating. He talked about his work and about the transition from work to school after being away from the books for awhile. "For the last two years my life consisted solely of work and school. Tell me about you, Matt."

Matt looked down at his plate. "There really isn't much to tell. I work at a small town bank." He wanted to talk about Kent, but he didn't want to say too much.

"Anyone special in your life, Matt?"

Matt just couldn't go into his situation right now, but he hated to lie. "Not really." Matt was surprised to hear his own words.

"Well, like I said, for the last two years it has been work and school for me, Matt."

Matt smiled, but then stopped suddenly. Smiling made his face hurt.

"Well, how about a drink back at the house?"

"That sounds great." Once again, Matt's words were out of his mouth before he could stop them.

Matt felt comfortable at Dustin's house and he felt comfortable with Dustin. Dustin sat down beside Matt on the sofa. "So, about that someone special, what does 'not really' mean?"

"I guess sometimes I just don't know where I stand."

"I see. Where do you want to stand?"

Matt wished he had answers for this nice man who shared his life's passion. "I don't know that, either. I'm sorry, Dustin."

"No apology needed. We've all been there."

The two of them talked awhile longer, about their work mostly. "Would you like to tour my bank tomorrow after the morning's conference?"

Matt's eyes brightened. "I would. Thank you."

Dustin and Matt set their empty glasses down and stood up at the same time. They were face to face when they stood up, and Matt felt his heart beat faster. "I should probably get back to the hotel."

Dustin nervously cleared his throat. He would have given anything to kiss Matt, but he would never break up a serious couple, if that was what Matt was a part of. "Yes, tomorrow will be here before we know it." Dustin casually placed his hand lightly on Matt's back without thinking about it, and Matt stiffened. Once inside Dustin's car, Matt relaxed. He had liked the feeling of Dustin's hand on his back, but he knew that he shouldn't have liked it. Dustin dropped him off at the hotel, and said, "I will see you bright and early tomorrow. You will love my bank. Listen to me, my bank," he said with a laugh.

Matt smiled. "I'm sure I will."

Dustin watched as Matt walked inside the old hotel, wishing that he knew more about him, and more importantly, wondering how he had gotten the bruise on his face that he had noticed when they were face to face in his house, and which Matt had been trying to hide.

Matt walked into his hotel suite and looked out at the mountains again. "It is going to be really hard to leave this place," he said aloud. He took a shower and lay in bed. He thought about Dustin and how much fun they had had today and then he thought of Kent. He would be at work now, but Matt needed to call him. They hadn't spoken since he had left Sunday morning. I have to remember to call him tomorrow before I go to Dustin's bank, he decided. He watched a little television and then fell asleep.

Matt awoke again to his friendly wakeup call. How long did I sleep? he wondered. He knew that it was almost midnight when he had finally fallen asleep. He couldn't remember the last time he had slept for eight hours straight. He stretched and got ready for the conference.

"You look well rested. Guess the skiing didn't hurt you too much."

"No. I feel great, Dustin. It must be the air up here. I've really never slept better."

"Well, glad to hear it." Dustin wondered if the bruise on Matt's face, which today had been freshly covered, had something to do with Matt sleeping better out here away from home and he guessed that it did.

Matt listened intently as the group of bankers was treated to a visit by the chairman of the Federal Reserve. Dustin noticed the light in Matt's eyes that seemed to shine more brightly every day. That light had not been present when Dustin had first met him.

"Interesting conference today," Dustin commented. "You must like the international aspects of banking."

"I do. I wish I had had more time to take a few more classes in international finance and management, but I told myself that could wait for graduate school some day," Matt admitted.

"But you decided that graduate school wasn't for you?"

"Oh, no, I wanted to go, but K...." Matt stopped.

"I'm sorry, you started to say something?" Dustin asked.

"Oh, I just thought that I should get some work experience before tackling a graduate degree."

"Well, are you ready to take a tour of a big city bank?" Dustin teased.

It was noon and Matt really needed to call Kent first. It had been two days since they had last spoken. Kent was no doubt seething with anger by now. "Do you mind if I make a call first?"

Dustin sensed that it was a personal call, so he offered to wait in the lobby. "Not at all, Matt. I'll pick us up some of the free books that were left in the conference room, compliments of the Federal Reserve. We have to get some of our tax dollars back somehow."

Matt smiled slightly and walked to the elevator, but the somewhat nervous look in his eyes did not go unnoticed by Dustin. Matt dialed his home number the minute he walked into the suite. "Speak," Kent's voice answered.

"Kent, I'm glad you're home," Matt said in as upbeat a tone as he possibly could.

"Why haven't you called, Matt? Too busy with your 'colleagues'? You couldn't even find the time to say goodbye on Sunday?"

"I'm sorry, Kent. I left you a note. I didn't want to wake you."

Kent said nothing.

"So, how are things going back home?"

"Nothing exciting. I painted some on Sunday."

"That's nice. I'm sure it looks great. I can't wait to see it."

"Yeah, well, don't expect it to be finished by the time you get back. I do have a job, you know. I don't have the time for jet setting across the country like you do."

Matt didn't know what to say to Kent. He never did know what to say when he began to belittle himself like he was doing now. "Well, I have to get back to the conference now, Kent. I love you."

"You'll be home on Friday?"

"That's right. I can't wait to see you."

"Yeah, me too," Kent said, his tone softening a little.

Matt hung up the phone and closed his eyes. He felt tense again, which had seemed to fade since being here. He locked the door and met Dustin in the lobby.

Dustin could see the worry lines in Matt's face that had not been present yesterday. "Here you go," he said, handing Matt a stack of books from the conference. "These don't take the place of graduate school, but they do look pretty interesting."

Matt thanked him and tried to get the phone call to Kent out of his mind, at least for the time being. He would buy something for Kent while he was here. That would make him feel better.

Dustin noticed Matt's faraway look, but he didn't want to pry. "This is it. This is what I like to call 'my bank'." Dustin laughed at himself, and so did Matt. He couldn't help it. Dustin's enthusiasm was infectious.

"Your bank has more than one story, Dustin. You've got me beat."

Dustin walked into his bank and was warmly welcomed. "Hey, aren't you supposed to be somewhere?" "You aren't just out playing around now, are you?" They teased Dustin just like they teased John back home. "I am all work," Dustin said, defending himself. Now he even sounds like John, Matt thought. "This is Matt, a fellow conference virgin."

Matt looked down for a second, embarrassed. He smiled, and hoped that his face hadn't turned bright red.

Dustin proudly showed off his bank to Matt. Although it was a big city bank to Matt, it had the feel of a small town bank. Dustin introduced Matt to the vice president, who was much older than Dustin. Matt wondered how the older man felt about working for someone as young as Dustin, but Dustin showed the man the greatest respect. "Tom has taught me so much, Matt. I wouldn't have made it without him. I would have quit after my first week if it hadn't been for Tom." Tom just shook his head, but Matt knew that Dustin had meant what he said.

It was two in the afternoon when Matt and Dustin left the bank. "How about lunch? This is the perfect time for lunch," Dustin offered.

"Okay, but this time it's on me, or my boss, rather. He has given me carte blanche with his expense account, and as generous as he is, he would be disappointed if I didn't take advantage at least a little."

Dustin looked at Matt. "Lunch is on John, then," Dustin announced, as they left the building.

Dustin took Matt to a small café not far from his house. "I eat here quite often. I can come in here in jeans or I can come in here dressed in a suit and tie. This is one place where people actually come for the food. It is the best."

Matt had never been impressed with fancy restaurants. He much preferred the cozy and comfy settings of small cafés.

"Nothing fancy here, Matt. Sandwiches and soups."

"That sounds great, Dustin." Matt took one bite of his sandwich, and Dustin smiled.

"See what I mean?"

"This is the best," Matt concurred.

"I think their secret ingredient is basil," Dustin said with a smile. Matt wasn't sure if he was joking or not, but he didn't care either. He was hungry and the food was delicious. "Well, I hate to see you go back to that stuffy old hotel so soon. Come on back to the house for awhile."

Matt agreed. He wasn't ready to leave Dustin yet.

"You can see that not much has changed since yesterday," Dustin informed as they walked into his house.

"I doubt if your house ever looks messy, Dustin. It's beautiful."

Dustin smiled. "At the risk of sounding like an alcoholic, would you care for a glass of wine?"

"Love one," Matt said with a laugh. "And I don't think of you as an alcoholic," he added.

"One drink a day is about all I can handle, if that much," Dustin assured him. "What do you think of Denver, Matt?"

"It's beautiful. I love the view of the mountains, but what I have noticed more than anything is how much better I sleep out here than I do at home. It must be the thinner air."

Dustin knew that this was his chance to say what he thought, and that if he didn't do it now, he never would. "Perhaps there is less stress here," Dustin said, looking right at Matt.

"I do have quite a drive each day and long work days."

"How much sleep do you get, Matt?"

"Depends. Most nights I get enough."

Dustin somehow doubted that.

"Why do you ask?"

"If you don't mind my saying, Matt, when I first met you it appeared to me that you had a mark under one eye, perhaps what we like to call 'bags' from too little sleep?" Matt carelessly touched his eye. Had Dustin noticed the bruise? Did he suspect? "It seems to be going away the longer you are here."

"Oh," Matt said, not offering anything further.

Dustin could no longer ignore his own desires. He set Matt's wine glass down with his own. He gently ran a finger along Matt's lips, collecting the wine that lingered there. He kissed the wine from his finger and then pressed his finger to Matt's lips. Matt closed his eyes. His lips parted automatically. He wanted Dustin to kiss him. He wanted Dustin to take him to places that he had never been before. He felt the heat of Dustin's breath as it neared his lips. Dustin's arm around him caused Matt to gasp. Then he felt the gentle touch of Dustin's lips on his own and he could not resist. He did not want to resist Dustin.

His arms went around Dustin, holding him, welcoming his body to his own. Dustin pulled back slightly and Matt slowly opened his eyes. Dustin whispered, "Do I need to stop, Matt? I will if you want me to."

Matt could barely speak. "No," he said. He continued to hold Dustin, and Dustin kissed Matt again. His kisses were gentle, yet passionate and sensual. Dustin had not planned this and he had no idea where he planned to go from here. He knew that there was someone at home waiting for Matt. Matt had made enough slips to give that much away. Dustin also suspected that the mark and puffiness under Dustin's eye was not from lack of sleep. But who could possibly hurt this sweet man he was now holding in his arms? Dustin stopped kissing Matt so that he could catch his breath. He rested his head on Matt's shoulder, his hot breath sweeping across Matt's neck. "Where do we go from here, Matt?"

Matt swept his hand through Dustin's thick hair. He knew he should stop, but he didn't want to stop. He wanted to know what it was like to make love with someone who did not anger as easily as Kent. He needed to know if what he had with Kent was love. Was it a love facsimile? "Don't stop," he heard himself whisper.

Dustin stood up and led Matt by the hand around the corner and down the long hallway to his bedroom. The sun was beginning to disappear behind the mountains and its subdued rays cast romantic hues of light through Dustin's window. Matt had no idea how this should go. He had only been with one man. Dustin lay on the bed and welcomed Matt to join him. Matt hoped that Dustin did not sense his hesitancy, but he did. "Let me love you tonight," he said, and Matt lay down beside him. Dustin held him and kissed him. He undressed Matt, touching him as if he wanted to know every inch of him. When Matt was completely naked, Dustin backed up just a little, and Matt tried to cover himself. Dustin held his hand to stop him. "You're beautiful, Matt. All of you is beautiful."

Dustin began to undress himself, but Matt stopped him. "Let me," he whispered. Dustin closed his eyes so that Matt could touch him as he pleased. Matt rolled Dustin's nipples between his fingers, and he watched as Dustin's cock began to respond to his touch. "Kiss me, Matt," Dustin whispered.

Matt first kissed Dustin's nipples before kissing his lips. Matt was bringing pleasure to every part of Dustin's body, awakening in him feelings that had lain dormant for too many years. Dustin held Matt to him, and then he rolled Matt onto his back. "Tell me, Matt. What do you like?"

Matt looked at Dustin, somewhat confused by the question. Kent had always been a demanding lover, but Dustin was very different from Kent. Dustin had asked him what he liked and what he wanted. Matt looked into Dustin's eyes. His sincerity was real, not faked. Dustin held Matt's balls in his hand and Matt parted his legs. He continued to look into Matt's eyes as he awakened his most erotic senses. Matt moaned. Dustin kissed his lips. Dustin pulled the lobe of one ear into his mouth and whispered, "Let me bring you to orgasm."

Matt felt his cock twitch from Dustin's sultry words. He closed his eyes and allowed his body the physical pleasure that it craved. Dustin swept his tongue lightly across Matt's fully erect cock. "Ohh," Matt moaned. Dustin fondled Matt's balls and let a finger slide downward and stroke beneath and behind Matt's balls. Dustin slid his tongue upward and around Matt's cock. Matt's body completely surrendered to the man's touch. Dustin held the top of Matt's cock between his lips while he laid his tongue flat across the head to capture the drops that were waiting to fall. Matt opened his eyes halfway and watched as Dustin made love to every part of his body. "Dustin," he said, and then closed his eyes. When Dustin was certain that Matt's body was ready, he intensified the pleasure that he had been giving until Matt was grabbing Dustin's thick head of hair as he felt his climax nearing. "Dustin," he said again. Matt gasped, then moaned, and then he came hard as Dustin gave his body the pleasure that it had not yet known. Dustin was in no hurry for Matt's climax to end. He wanted Matt to know no end to the pleasure that he could give him and the pleasure that he deserved.

Dustin lay beside Matt and held him. Matt opened his eyes and looked down at Dustin. What did Dustin now expect from him in return? Did he want what Kent had always wanted? "Dustin, what can I do for you?"

Dustin looked up at Matt. "What do you like to do?"

Matt closed his eyes. His mind went back to what Kent had always demanded and how it had made him feel afterward. "I will do whatever you want," he answered, with a slightly hesitant look on his face.

Dustin kissed Matt's arm. "No, baby, that isn't how it should be. Never change you for me or for anyone else." He winked at Matt, and Matt's heart melted.

Matt looked at Dustin's cock and he wanted it in his mouth. "I like the same thing," Matt said in a soft voice.

"You got it," Dustin said. Dustin loved the warmth of Matt's tongue and mouth on his erect cock. He showed Matt and he told Matt how much pleasure he was giving him and he meant every word and every movement. Matt brought Dustin more pleasure than he had known in a very long time. "Oh, baby," Dustin moaned as he climaxed with Matt's lovemaking.

Matt lay beside Dustin with his hand on Dustin's leg. He thought about Kent and what the two of them shared. He wasn't sure if they really shared anything any longer. If they did, why was he here with another man? Am I trying to find a way out of my situation? That couldn't be it. He tried to convince himself that he was simply curious to know what sex with someone else was like.

"You okay?" Dustin asked.

Matt looked up at him. "I'm better than okay," he half lied. Matt was more confused now than he had been before he and Dustin had made love. The two of them lay together for awhile longer. Matt was almost asleep when he looked up at Dustin's closed eyes. "Dustin, I should probably get back to the hotel."

"Oh, yes, of course. Tell me I didn't fall asleep."

Matt smiled. "You didn't fall asleep."

Dustin laughed his infectious laugh. They both knew that he had fallen asleep. Dustin left Matt at the hotel with his usual cheery, "I will see you bright and early." He held Matt's hand until their hands slowly slid apart.

The next morning after once again sleeping so soundly that his wakeup call woke him before his alarm did, Matt met Dustin in the lobby. Dustin lightly placed an arm around Matt and said quietly, "You okay about yesterday?"

Matt smiled, which quickly became a grin. "I'm fine."

The next two days were longer than the first two, with the conference unexpectedly lasting until mid afternoon. Dustin and Matt had time for dinner and a drink each evening, but nothing more. On Friday, when the conference ended at noon, Dustin offered to drive Matt to the airport. "Okay," Matt said, eagerly. He knew that he would miss Dustin once he was gone. He missed him already.

Before Dustin left Matt at the airport, he and Matt sat in Dustin's car and talked for a few minutes. "Matt, this is for you," Dustin said, and he handed Matt a card with several phone numbers written on it.

"What's this?"

"You can reach me at anytime from anywhere. Keep this card in a safe place."

Matt looked at the card and then he looked at Dustin.

"May I call you at work, Matt, when you are at the bank?"

"Of course," Matt said, happy that Dustin wanted to stay in contact with him. He wrote down both the main number at the bank as well as the direct number to his office.

Dustin leaned over and kissed Matt. He took his hand in his, folding his fingers with Matt's. Looking directly into Matt's eyes, he finally said what he had waited all week to say. "If you ever need someplace to stay or someone to talk to, you are always welcome in my home, Matt." He gently touched Matt's cheek where the bruise had been. "I would hate to lose you, Matt."

Matt's eyes were fixed on Dustin's obviously all seeing and all knowing eyes. He almost hated to return to his former life of loneliness and very little sleep. He looked at Dustin's hand holding his tightly. "I'd better get going," he said.

"I know, Matt. I know." Dustin gently pressed his lips to Matt's cheek, the cheek where the bruise had been, and then he gently kissed Matt's hand. Matt swallowed hard. They said goodbye in the parking lot and Dustin watched as the huge airport swallowed the man he had known for only a little while. He waited for nearly thirty minutes before driving away, hoping that Matt would come running back to him, but knowing that he would not.

Matt looked at the card that Dustin had given him and tucked it away in his wallet. He stared down at the clouds below him as the plane coursed across the Colorado skies. When the plane landed, Matt was tired and not looking forward to a two hour drive home. He thought of Dustin the entire time and felt that all familiar knot begin to form in his stomach as the remote back roads brought him closer and closer to his home and to the life that he had built with Kent.

It was Friday evening and Kent should have been at work, but when Matt pulled into the driveway, Kent's car was there. It was seven in the evening. Why was Kent here? Matt took a deep breath and rolled his suitcases into the house. The television was blaring and Matt had been looking forward to a quiet evening alone. "Kent?" Matt knew that he couldn't have been heard over the deafening loudness of the television. Matt set down his things and walked into the den. "I'm home, Kent," he said, trying to be cheery.

Kent muted the television. "I expected you to be home hours ago," he said.

"I told you what time my plane got in, Kent. Then I had a two hour drive home." Matt walked into the bedroom, feeling beaten down already, and Kent followed him.

"So I suppose that it's my fault, then. I should have been at the airport waiting for you, right?"

Matt did not need to come home to this, not tonight. "No, Kent, I'm not blaming anyone. Planes land when they land."

Kent walked over and forced his way between the bed and Matt. "What's wrong, Kent?"

"What's wrong? What's wrong? I traded my Sunday so that I could be home today and as late as it is now, I may as well have worked. Now I have to work seven days straight because of you." On the last three words, Kent shoved Matt hard against the wall.

Matt braced himself to avoid hitting his head. "Kent, I'm sorry. I should have taken an earlier flight, but the conference wasn't over until noon."

"The conference, the conference, that's all I've heard about lately, the conference."

Matt knew that he had not bragged about his job ever and he certainly had not bragged about the conference, and having been gone for a week he had no idea where Kent's anger was coming from. "What's really wrong, Kent?"

Kent slapped Matt hard across the face. "You think I'm lying about something, Matt? You are the hotshot banker man who has been jet setting across the friendly skies. Are you a member of the Mile High Club now?"

Matt felt dizzy. He hadn't eaten since lunch and the slap on his face hadn't helped matters. "No, Kent," he said calmly.

"I don't believe you, you filthy liar."

Matt saw the fist coming, but he did not move fast enough to miss the punch.

Kent looked at Matt's body on the floor. "Get up, bitch," he screamed, but Matt did not hear him. Kent kicked Matt twice in the stomach, but Matt did not move. "Fuck. Is he dead?" Kent could see the rise and fall of Matt's chest. "Matt?" Kent had no idea what to do. Panicked, he dragged Matt's body to the car. He drove as fast as he could to the small town where Matt worked. "Think, Kent, what should I do?" He took Matt to the hospital and told the biggest lie that he could think of. "I found this man on the side of the road. I was coming home from work. Is he dead?"

The emergency room physician assured Kent that Matt was not dead and that he had done the right thing by picking him up. "I'm afraid I can't stay," Kent lied.

"I understand. You did a good thing today. I didn't get your name?"

Kent walked away. "It's not important," he said.

Matt slowly came around while in the hospital bed. His face was bruised, and after the physician saw the kick marks on his stomach, he realized that Matt had been beaten by someone. The doctor didn't know the man who had brought Matt into the emergency room, but he did know Matt. Matt was one of the nicest guys he knew. He was always friendly when he saw the doctor in the bank. Who would do this to him?

"Matt?"

Matt slowly opened his eyes.

"Matt, it's Dr. Kingsley. Can you hear me?"

Matt tried to focus on the doctor.

"Matt, do you remember what happened?"

Matt closed his eyes, and the events of the day slowly came back to him.

"A man brought you in tonight, Matt. He said that he found you on the side of the road on his way home from work. He didn't give his name."

Matt tried to think. Did he have a wreck on his way home from the airport? Matt was stable, so Dr. Kingsley asked everyone to leave the room. He then sat down next to Matt on the bed. "Matt, there are two bruises on your stomach that appear to be from kicks and a pretty good shiner under your left eye."

Matt slowly reached a hand to his face. It hurt really badly, much worse than the last one. "Matt, can you tell me exactly what happened? Do you remember anything?"

Matt held his head. He remembered the hit, but not the kicks. Did Kent drive him here? "Who brought me in?"

Dr. Kingsley repeated what he had told Matt earlier. "The man did not give us his name, Matt. He indicated that he had found you by the side of the road on his way home from work." The doctor described the man to Matt, and Matt closed his eyes. Kent did not find me by the road, he thought. He did not work today, either. He must have kicked me while I was passed out, he thought, feeling sick. "Matt, we had to positively identify you, so we went through your wallet. We found a card with the name of Dustin Marks written on it along with a few phone numbers. We did contact Mr. Marks. He informed us that he lives in Denver. Is that correct?"

"Yes," Matt said.

"Mr. Marks was extremely concerned about you, Matt. He is on a plane on his way here as we speak and he should be here around midnight. Do you want me to call John from the bank?"

"Not tonight, okay?"

"Whatever you like, Matt. Try to get some rest."

Matt didn't remember falling asleep, but when he opened his eyes again Dustin was sitting on his bed holding his hand. "Dustin?" he whispered.

"I'm here, Matt. I'm here."

"Thanks for coming."

"I wouldn't be anywhere else, Matt."

"Don't you want to know what happened?"

"I know what happened, Matt. I've been where you are."

A look of shock and disbelief spread across Matt's face. "Surprised, Matt?"

"But you seem so strong and so sure of yourself, Dustin. You don't seem weak like me."

Dustin laughed his usual infectious laugh. "You are definitely not weak, Dustin."

"Sure," Matt said, disbelief in his voice.

"You love someone who does not love himself. We must first love ourselves before we can truly love someone else."

"You were like me, Dustin?"

"Yes, Matt. It was a long time ago, my first year in college. I thought I could change him by loving him, but that's not the way it works, is it?"

Matt shook his head. "Contrary to all those silly love songs, it takes a lot more than love to make a relationship work," Dustin added.

"I guess I felt responsible for his unhappiness somehow, Dustin."

"Sneaks up on you. It's a very lonely existence, though, isn't it, the shame, not being able to talk to anyone about what is going on at home?"

Matt nodded.

"During those years, Matt, I did the same two things day after day. I went to school and then I came straight home to him, Matt. I saw no one, talked to no one, except him. I felt as if I were walking on pins and needles for nearly two years, not knowing what to say or not say to him."

"You knew, didn't you, Dustin? You knew where I had gotten my bruise."

Dustin nodded. He knew.

Matt closed his eyes. He felt like crying, but no tears would come. "You loved him, didn't you, Dustin?"

"Absolutely, Matt. I think a part of me will always love him, but I had to make a choice. It took me a long, long time to realize that. I thought that every couple was like us, but they aren't, Matt. I didn't see that until I began to break away. I talked to other couples, interacted with them, and discovered that I was the one who was in the 'different' relationship. I wanted what those other couples had." Dustin sighed. "I'm not going to tell you that it was easy leaving him, because it was not. I was too much a part of the relationship to be able to see it for what it really was. You know the old saying, 'You can't see the forest for the trees'?" Matt nodded. "It's like that, Matt. I couldn't see the whole picture, or the forest, because I was a part of the whole picture, or too close to the trees."

"What do I do, Dustin?"

"That, my dear man, is a decision that only you can make."

"I wouldn't mind getting that graduate degree," Matt admitted.

"Denver has great schools, Matt. I know someone who could use a roommate."

Matt studied this knowing and kind face. "Roommate, Dustin?"

"Roommate, lover, whatever you like."

"What if we don't work out?"

"Then we move on, Matt, plain and simple. No hard feelings. For now, though, I would love to have you with me."

Matt needed to sleep.

"I will be in the lobby, Matt. See you bright and early."
Matt smiled.

"Bright and early," Matt repeated. He loved those words. Those were Dustin's words.

Once Matt had healed, on the outside anyway, he gave his two weeks' notice at the bank. His boss and mentor for years gave him the most lavish party his small town had ever known.

"I think the entire town is here, John."

"Well, I should hope so," John had said with his usual cheer.

Matt also gave two weeks' notice to Kent, and he stayed with John and his family until Kent had moved out.

Matt sold his house and caught the first plane to Denver. Wanting to surprise Dustin, he arrived a day earlier than he had promised and had taken a cab to Dustin's house. He rang the doorbell and he heard Dustin's familiar voice, "It's open." Matt walked inside and tried to be very quiet so that he could surprise Dustin. He heard the soft jazz that Dustin liked coming from the bedroom. He set his things down and walked down the long hallway to Dustin's bedroom where the music was playing softly. Dustin was in the bathroom and didn't see Matt until he walked back into the bedroom. "Is this a mirage?"

"No, this is real," Matt assured him.

Dustin wrapped his arms around Matt, holding Dustin's cute little butt in his hands. Then he kissed him with passion and hunger. "I have dreamed of this moment," he said, barely taking the time to stop kissing.

"Make love to me, Dustin, please."

Dustin led Matt to his big bed and laid him down. They undressed each other, touching and kissing each other as if they had been apart for years.

Matt couldn't wait for the taste of Dustin's cock.

"Oh, Matt," Dustin gasped.

"It's been too long, Dustin. I'm hungry."

"We can't have that," Dustin said, welcoming the lips of his lover on his erection. Dustin eased Matt's cute little butt up and over him, and he seductively sucked Matt's hot cock down into his mouth.

Matt had to stop to catch his breath after Dustin's erotic surprise. "Dustin," he moaned. Matt touched and stroked Dustin and Dustin offered himself completely to his lover. They made love until they were both exhausted.

Matt fell into Dustin's welcoming open arms and slept soundly once again in the cool thin mountain air.

Brass Knuckles

Rick Mason is on a mission and his mission is the Mafia, the Mafioso, and specifically, the Giaconi Family, one of the most powerful Mafia families to have ever immigrated to the United States. Lucian, the elusive boss of the Giaconi Family, has escaped the authorities for decades. His manipulative means and ruthless ways have allowed him to control any and all he chooses, and the unfortunate souls who dare cross him end up at the bottom of the murky waters of the Muddy Mo; that is, the Mississippi River, and a few have become tasty treats for the hungry alligators that can always be found lurking not far from the city the Giaconi Family calls home; The Big Easy, New Orleans, Louisiana. When the car of Lucian Giaconi's son-in-law is pulled from the Mississippi River with no body inside, Rick is determined to find out exactly what happened to the man, and he will do whatever it takes to stop the elusive crime boss, "Never Lose Lucian", once and for all.

"Shh, keep it down. You never know who might be out here watching us. You want somebody to hear us? Now, lower it down slowly. How much cement you get in there?" "Plenty." "There, now push it on down with your foot."

The two men stood at the edge of the Pauline Street Wharf and watched as the chest made of pure cedar drifted slowly downward into the Mississippi River. "How long you think it'll take 'til it's out in the Gulf?" "About half a day, if it gets that far." The two men laughed as they watched the cedar chest disappear from their sight as it was swallowed up by the murky waters of the Mississippi River.

They looked around them. It was just after midnight. They headed back to the warehouse where the Giaconi Cedar Furniture was made.

"Lucian will be pleased," Johnny said.

"Yes, yes he will be," Sammy agreed.

Sammy "the snake" Malini and Johnny "JoJo" Galioso had worked for Lucian Giaconi since they were in their teens. They had first worked for the old man, Lucian, Sr., and now they worked for his son, Lucian, Jr. They didn't think that the son could possibly be more ruthless than the old man, but time had proven them wrong, very wrong.

Sammy and JoJo drove the short distance to the warehouse, parked their dark vehicle in the back, and walked slowly to the door. Sammy tapped twice with his hand down at his side, the secret code, and the door opened. The security camera allowed Lucian's son, Jeff, otherwise known as the Underboss, to see that it was them waiting outside. The doors opened and the two men walked inside. The door closed and locked behind them.

"All done, Jeff."

"It was a success?"

"Yes, success," Sammy informed him.

"No one says a word to Cheri. As far as anyone knows, Pierre got drunk and drove his car into the river."

The two men nodded, and then left the building. They were both thinking the same thing, though neither said a word, not even to each other. But if Lucian could have his own son-in-law taken out, he wouldn't hesitate to do it to them.

Sammy dropped JoJo off at his house in Metairie and then drove to his own house in Kenner. Sammy's wife was sleeping soundly when he crawled quietly into bed. She would never know. She knew what Sammy did for a living and otherwise, but she had a beautiful home worth at least half a million dollars and could buy anything she wanted. She and JoJo's wife were good friends, which helped maintain solidarity within the family. Nothing was ever said between the two of them about the business. They had both grown up in New Orleans and both knew the guys who were connected and who could give them the best time. Most importantly, they knew that if they ever talked about the family, even amongst themselves, they would be next to be laid to rest at the bottom of the Mississippi or fed to the hungry alligators that roamed the swamplands that surrounded the city.

Jeff stayed at the warehouse a little while longer, waiting for the call that he knew would come. The phone rang at exactly 1:00 a.m. "Yeah, it's done. Went off without a problem. See you tomorrow, Dad."

Jeff hung up the phone and locked the door of the warehouse on his way out. He didn't have far to drive. He lived in the Garden District of New Orleans, just a few blocks from his father's house.

From his rented room on the top floor of the old hotel, agent Rick Mason had watched the two men submerge the cedar chest. Unfortunately, he had not seen what was in it. Damn, he thought. If only I had access to the warehouse or knew someone who did.

Rick Mason had been working for years to get close to the Giaconi family, and now he had located the city of its elusive boss. It was New Orleans, not Chicago as he had once thought. Chicago had been a decoy set up very carefully by the owners of Giaconi Pizza. The two families were connected somehow, but Rick didn't know exactly how. He suspected that Lucian Giaconi was the head of both; that they were really just one family, and not two, which was originally suspected among the Feds.

Rick Mason had studied the intricacies of organized crime for years and he knew very well how their cover-ups worked. The idea was to keep as many layers between the head of the family, the boss, and the actual crimes committed as they possibly could. Let the lowest layer do the dirty work and it kept the focus off of the top. That way, the family's business was not disturbed and could continue uninterrupted.

Rick had also watched Jeff as he walked to his car after leaving the warehouse. He had gotten a good look at him and had also gotten an image of him with his digital equipment especially made for night imaging. "Well, that's a start," he said aloud. He put his equipment away for the night, and studied the photo of Jeff Giaconi. "Hm, black hair, dark eyes, about 5'10", 5'11", nice build, well toned, very nice ass," he thought. Jeff fit the description of the man that Rick dreamed of meeting someday.

Rick made a quick call to his boss describing what he had seen and sadly what he hadn't seen, and then went to bed.

The alarm went off beside Rick's head and he reached over to turn it off. He opened his eyes. He picked up the picture of Jeff that he had taken last night. "If I can just get close to Jeff," he thought. "Maybe I could blow the lid off of this crime family and their lawless ways."

Rick had heard through the grapevine that Jeff Giaconi was not the ruthless thug that his father was. It was rumored that Jeff had even tried to leave the family business a couple of times and had been taught a lesson and had been given a not-so-friendly reminder that he should never try this again both times that he had tried to leave and had been returned to his father. That was the main reason that Jeff now lived only four houses from his father. Lucian knew that he needed to keep an eye on his youngest son. Lucian had been watching last night when Jeff pulled into his drive. Jeff was watched day and night by someone, if not by Lucian himself.

Rick studied the image of Jeff. It was somewhat blurred, but he had gotten a good enough image to keep it in his mind.

He turned on the television and sure enough, they were reporting the accidental death of one of the city's well known attorneys, Pierre Moran. It was reported that the man's car had somehow skidded or swerved off of the road and into the Mississippi River in the vicinity of the Pauline Street Wharf. The news video was showing skid marks and Mr. Moran's car being pulled out earlier this morning. How convenient, and how very genius, thought Rick. Damn, they thought of everything. The news reporter continued with, "The windows of the vehicle had apparently been rolled down and it was apparent that Mr. Moran's body had somehow been carried out into the Gulf." Oh, man. They plan everything down to the letter. If only I had seen the actual body being placed inside the chest, Rick said to himself.

Rick continued to watch the news report as they gave the name of Pierre Moran's wife, Cheri, and their daughter, Asaria. Arrangements were pending. "Closed casket for sure," Rick laughed, as he commented. "If it wasn't so sick, it would have been funny to hear all the lies spewed by the almighty Giaconi clan.

Rick realized that the only way to the head of the family was through the youngest son, Jeff. He was the weak link, and he had wanted out. He had wanted out so badly that he had risked his life and had tried to leave the family, twice.

Rick took out his equipment and positioned it so that he could see the warehouse again and then waited for someone to show up. It was early and the only people he had seen so far were the factory workers. If only I could get a good look around inside the warehouse, he thought. He continued to watch, hoping to get a glimpse of the two men that he could just barely see last night and hopefully Jeff Giaconi.

Rick picked up his cell phone to call his boss. "What do you think, Bill?" he asked. Rick's boss was a great guy. He trusted Rick to use his own judgment. The agency was so thin now because of budget cuts that Bill was busy with his own undercover work. He didn't have the time or the desire to micromanage.

"I'd say you're right on track, Rick. Stick with the kid like glue. See where he goes for lunch. He's got to leave the warehouse sometime."

"Will do, Bill." Rick put his cell phone in his jeans pocket. He always used his cell phone. Not as easy to trace.

Rick never left his rented room without putting everything in the locked cabinet he had brought with him. He never knew who might be onto him. He thought about going out for breakfast, but he didn't want to miss seeing anything at the Giaconi Warehouse. He called down to the lobby of the old hotel and had his breakfast brought up. When it arrived, he opened the door just enough to take it from the woman, tipped her, and then closed and locked the door behind her. For all Rick knew, the hotel could be owned by the Giaconi family. They owned a few restaurants here in New Orleans and also had a lot of interest in the casino business that seemed to have sprung up overnight along the Gulf Coast.

While he waited for something to happen at Giaconi Furniture, Rick read the information he had on the family. The Giaconi family had immigrated to the United States from Naples in the 1920s. They had first settled in Chicago and New Orleans and from there had migrated west, but the main family lived right here in The Big Easy. Rick still did not quite know how the two families had split or why, but he had a feeling that there was some connection between the Chicago and New Orleans Giaconi families. Rick had spent a few years in Chicago and had come up with nothing, so he knew the answers had to be here in New Orleans. He read further, but the information offered little other than after feeling that they had somehow been denied the American dream, they had done what many others had done during those troubled economic times and had sought to make their own dreams a reality through illegal means. "It's not illegal until you get caught, I guess," Rick said to himself. "They are making a lot of money without paying taxes."

"Here we go," Rick said, as he watched Jeff Giaconi arrive at the warehouse. Jeff got out of his car, put his suit jacket on, and walked inside the building. "He's alone. That's good." Rick had spoken too soon. Right behind Jeff was Lucian, who pulled up in what looked to Rick to be a Lexus, new and shiny, not a scratch or dent on it. "Figures," he said. "He would probably kill first, and ask questions later, if someone dented his car." Rick tried to zoom in on the elusive don of the Giaconi family. He had never seen him before today. "Looks just like he stepped out of the 1950s. Typical mafia attire." Lucian walked to the door of his business wearing dark glasses and a large dark hat, and dressed to the nines. "Laughable. Does the man own a mirror?" Rick almost laughed out loud.

Rick kept his eyes on the warehouse. He hadn't seen Sammy or JoJo arrive yet. He waited all day for something to happen. Finally, when it was almost dark, he said aloud, "Okay, here's my break." He watched as Jeff Giaconi got into his car alone and pulled out of the parking lot. Rick had seen the old man leave a few hours ago. "Now's my chance," he said, and locked up his belongings and headed out to follow the youngest son of Lucian.

Rick had Jeff on his car's specialized radar and the signal indicated that he was heading toward the hotel. "Good, he's coming straight to me," he said. Rick remained in his car and continued to watch Jeff's car on his radar. Then he watched as Jeff's vehicle pulled into the parking lot of the hotel. "What is he doing here?" Rick began to feel nervous. He hoped they weren't onto him. They don't own this place, do they? If they do, it's bugged for sure.

Rick drove quickly back to the hotel and mingled in the lobby. Jeff went into the restaurant of the hotel and was seated alone. Rick watched as the waitress removed the extra place setting from Jeff's table. He's alone tonight. That's good. Jeff's back was to Rick, so as far as Jeff knew Rick could have come in from outside the hotel just as he had.

Rick quickly went up to his room and changed into khaki pants and a polo shirt. He messed his hair a little so that it would appear as if he had come in from outside and then splashed on some cologne. "There. I look like any other tourist."

Rick walked into the restaurant and tried to appear lost, like a tourist might be. He walked up to Jeff, who was looking down at his menu.

"Excuse me, sir?"

Jeff looked up at Rick, and Rick almost melted. Jeff had the sweetest looking face he had ever seen. It looked pained somewhat, as if he were in anguish. But why wouldn't he be? Rick wanted to hold him, kiss him, pet him, take him somewhere away from his family and never let him go. Get a grip, Rick, he told himself. "Yes?" Jeff said.

"I think I'm lost," lied Rick.

"Oh, I've lived here all my life. Sit down. I can help you find anything."

Rick sat facing Jeff at the little table and fought the urge to hold his hand. Rick was fighting a lot of urges. He now had to think of a few places that he couldn't seem to find here in New Orleans. Thinking quickly, he said, "I was trying to find this address that I was given." He quickly scribbled a fake address and gave the piece of paper to Jeff.

"Hmm, I don't think I know that address," Jeff admitted. Jeff continued to stare at the address, trying to figure out where it was.

Rick looked at the man sitting across from him. God, he was gorgeous. Jeff studied Rick's face. To Jeff, Rick looked like a regular tourist. He was clean shaven, very waspy looking, definitely not Italian. Jeff would give almost anything to have been born into a non-mafia family. He was sick of the shady businesses of his father here in New Orleans and his uncle in Chicago. He was tired of being paranoid. He couldn't believe what his father had just done to his little sister's husband. If I could leave with this kind looking stranger, I would do it, he thought. Then he thought about the two times he had tried to leave before and he broke out in a sweat. He felt dizzy.

Rick had turned away, and when he looked back he saw a very different Jeff. Rick was out of his chair in an instant. "Hey, there, you don't look good. Here, bend down." Rick stood over Jeff and rubbed his back as the blood flowed back into his head. He poured some cold water on a napkin and wiped

Jeff's forehead and fanned him. Jeff felt better quickly and sat up.

"Thanks. I'm Jeff."

"Rick," he said. "You feeling better, Jeff?"

"A little, I guess. I think I'll get my food to go."

While the waitress wrapped Jeff's food, Rick offered, "I don't think you should drive, Jeff. I have a room in the hotel here. Would you like to come up? I promise you I'm not some weirdo or serial killer."

Jeff felt too weak to drive and too tired to argue. "Okay. Thanks."

Rick carried the food and helped Jeff to the elevator. Once inside his room, he helped Jeff to the bed. "Here, Jeff, rest awhile. You'll feel better soon." Rick was very glad that he had all of his stuff locked up. It could have blown everything if he hadn't. He poured cold water on a cloth and held it to Jeff's forehead. Jeff began to breathe more easily within minutes. Damn, the old man sure has done a number on this kid, Rick thought. Rick looked at Jeff. He looked so sweet, so young, and yet so very tired. Rick thought that Jeff looked to be in his early thirties, close to his own age. "Let me help you sit up, Jeff. You should eat something."

Rick helped Jeff sit up. He looked so tired, and he felt very weak.

"Ohh," Jeff groaned.

"Here, eat some of your dinner."

Jeff tried to sit up. Rick helped him lean against the pillows. Jeff picked up the fork and his hand shook. Rick got onto the bed beside him. "Here, Jeff. Let me help you." He cut a small piece of the grilled chicken and lifted it to Jeff's lips. Jeff looked at him. "Take a bite. It smells great."

Jeff opened his mouth and continued to watch this man he had just met. He had kind eyes. Jeff guessed him to be about the same age as he. He was tall and slender, with blondish-brown hair and bluish-gray eyes. His skin was an ivory color, unlike the olive and brown hues that graced his own. When you look like me, many people just assume that you are involved in organized crime in some way, Jeff thought bitterly. He accepted another bite from Rick. He is definitely not a part of my world, Jeff said to himself.

Jeff felt better after eating a few bites of the chicken.

Rick held the glass of water up to Jeff's lips and he took a drink.

Rick closed the takeout container and set it by the bed. "Better?"

"Yes, thanks." Jeff was looking at the television screen.

"You want to catch the news?"

Jeff nodded.

Rick walked over and turned on the television.

Breaking News was flashing across the screen. "This just in – It is confirmed that the drowning victim whose car was found along the Pauline Street Wharf last night was Pierre Moran, the son-in-law of the elusive mob boss, Lucian Giaconi. Services will be at the Saints Peter and Paul Catholic Church in Orleans Parish this Thursday at 10:00 a.m."

Rick looked at Jeff, who was obviously disturbed by the photos of the car being recovered from the river, the car that had been strategically placed to make Pierre's death look like an unfortunate accident. At least it bothers him. The kid's not made of stone like his father. "You okay, Jeff?"

"Yeah. I'd better be going. Thanks for everything, Rick."

Jeff sat up on the side of the bed. He leaned against the door for a second. Rick stood behind him and put his hand on his shoulder.

"Look, Jeff. You can come back here if you like. You know, to give me tips on how to get around in the city. I'm here for the week."

Jeff turned his head to look at Rick. There was something about him, but he couldn't figure out what it was. "Thanks," he said, and walked out the door. Damn, I hope he comes back, Rick said to himself.

This made no sense to Rick. How could he nail the Giaconi family if he and the kid were seen together? And Rick knew that Jeff was being closely watched at all times. He had been surprised to see him eating alone. He didn't think anyone had seen him here in the room, though. I hope not. Rick went to bed late that night. He had written some notes in his laptop and sent them to his boss.

The next morning Rick had an e-mail from his boss cautioning him to be careful with Jeff. "Try not to be seen out in public and if you think they know where you're staying, for God's sake get out of there." Rick clicked on the second entry. "Might not be a bad idea to be a fly on the wall at that funeral. Great way to get a look at the family." Rick had already thought of that, but it was good to get the go ahead from his boss.

Rick hadn't heard from Jeff since that one night a few nights ago, but he had hoped that after the funeral he might find time and a way to stop by some night.

Rick dressed for the funeral and parked a few blocks away from the church. He wore a dark suit, dark hat, and dark glasses. Hell, I look like one of them. He walked toward the church with his head down somewhat, looking around him. He was in a sea of black suits and black dresses. He sat in the back of the church so that he could see as many people as possible. When the family walked in behind the casket, which was empty of course, Rick got a good look at Pierre's widow, Cheri. She was sobbing, being escorted by her father. Jeff walked slowly behind, his head down, followed by the two men, Sammy and JoJo, who had disposed of the body that sinister night.

Rick was now determined more than ever to put Lucian Giaconi away. How could he be so cold and then play the part of the loving father? After the funeral, Rick kept his head down so that Jeff would not recognize him. He had no intention of going to the "burial." Even if there had been a body, what they did with the dead down here Rick found very creepy. Where I'm from, we bury our dead in the ground, he said to himself.

Rick was among the last to leave the church, but he had gotten a good look at some of the closest to Lucian, or at least who he thought were those closest to the man.

Rick hung up his suit and was in jeans and a t-shirt when he heard a knock on the door. He made sure his gun was locked in the drawer and he shoved the key in his pocket. He walked quietly to the door. "Yeah?"

"Rick, it's Jeff," he said quietly.

Rick backed up and unlocked the door. Jeff hurried inside without waiting to be asked. Rick locked the door behind him.

"I'm glad you came back. How have you been? Doing better?"

Jeff sat down on the bed. "Yeah, I'm fine. Thanks again."

"Take your shoes off, make yourself comfortable."

Jeff leaned against the headboard. Rick went to the other side of the bed and joined him.

"Need help finding anything?" he asked.

"I've been going through these brochures on the sites of the city, but can't decide which ones to see," he replied, flipping through the brochures.

Jeff looked at them. They sure made this city look squeaky clean. Carefully hidden was the major underground world with its corrupt government that truly ran the city. "Hm, guess it's all here," he said. Rick thought he detected a bit of sarcasm in Jeff's tone, but he couldn't be certain. Jeff continued to study the brochures as if he were seeing pictures of the city for the very first time.

Rick looked at him. He was so sweet looking. He was almost what could be described as a pretty man. His features weren't at all rugged, and they certainly didn't say "gangster." They were too fine.

Jeff set the brochures down and looked over at Rick. They looked at each other for awhile. Jeff looked straight ahead, pushed his hair back with his hand, and sighed. "I don't really know why I came here, Rick. You must think I'm weird or something. I barely know you." He looked back at Rick. "You could be a serial killer for all I know," he joked.

Rick laughed a little uneasily. "No, I can assure you that I'm no killer." He knew that he was looking at one, however. But he just couldn't see that in Jeff's eyes. They were too soft, too kind.

"Have a drink with me?" Jeff asked.

"Sure," Rick said. Poor guy probably drinks a lot, Rick thought. "I've got a bottle of Jack and some cola. It's pretty good, really," Rick offered. Rick poured them both a pretty stiff drink and handed a glass to Jeff. "It may not be as fancy as you're used to," he said.

"I don't need fancy, Rick. Sometimes simplicity is the real fancy stuff." Rick could see that in Jeff, could see that he didn't thirst for the material. Jeff almost gulped his drink and poured himself another. Rick drank about half of his as Jeff reached the halfway mark of his second. "I'm feeling a lot better now, Rick."

Jeff looked at Rick. Rick set his own glass down on the nightstand. Rick wasn't sure what he was seeing in Jeff's eyes, but he wanted to find out. "So, tell me Rick, are you married? I don't see a ring." Jeff was a lot different after a couple of drinks, much more talkative. The liquor seemed to give him the assertiveness he lacked without it.

"No, I'm not married, Jeff. I'm gay."

Rick watched for Jeff's reaction. So far, there was no reaction.

Jeff then set his glass down on the nightstand and laid his hand on Rick's. He looked at Rick. He was a stranger, and yet he wasn't. Rick smiled at him, not knowing what Jeff was looking for in him. Jeff moved closer to Rick, so close that Rick could smell the liquor on his breath and the cologne on his body.

In what was definitely a bold move for Jeff, he put his hand on Rick's face and gently kissed his lips. "Kiss me, Rick. Please don't push me away."

Rick knew he was in too deep now, if he wasn't before. He held Jeff as the sweet young man pressed his chest against his. Rick's hands moved up and down along Jeff's back as he welcomed Jeff's every kiss. Jeff's hands were in Rick's hair, on his face, and then down on his neck. His lips were on Rick's lips, Rick's cheek, the side of Rick's neck that was closest to him, but then he quickly returned to Rick's lips.

Jeff's hunger was as strong as Rick's, and neither was willing to stop. Jeff was pulling at Rick's t-shirt, eager to feel the hot flesh underneath, and Rick's body was quickly relenting to Jeff's touch. Jeff pulled Rick down onto the bed and forced the flimsy material of Rick's shirt upward. Rick had never been ravished like this, and he couldn't have stopped this sweet man if he had wanted to. He pulled Jeff's dress shirt out from where it had been neatly tucked inside his dress pants which he had worn to his brother-in-law's funeral and the two were moving with each other.

Jeff stopped kissing Rick just long enough to pull the t-shirt up and over Rick's head. "Rick," Jeff said quickly between breaths. "I want you, Rick," he finished, and grasped Rick firmly between the legs, forcing a moan from Rick's lips. Rick knew he should stop, but he couldn't. "Jeff," he tried to speak, but Jeff's mouth had his firmly within his own. Jeff was squeezing Rick's balls and trying to force his hand around to Rick's ass. He was trying to feel Rick through his jeans, and Rick's shorts were being pushed upward by the force of his hand.

Jeff's lips came off of Rick's lips with a hard force and he positioned his body to straddle Rick's, intent now on freeing the hardness that was trapped inside the tight denim of Rick's jeans. "Jeff, we should stop," Rick said, but he didn't want Jeff to stop. Jeff was stronger than Rick would have thought and with one move had forcibly pulled Rick's jeans to well below his knees.

Jeff was breathing so hard now that beads of sweat appeared on his forehead and on his chest. Rick slid his hand along Jeff's chest, wiping the sweat, and Jeff looked up at him. "I have to, Rick," he pleaded. Jeff's bulge was low and hard as it pushed against the smooth material of his dress pants. He pulled Rick's pants off completely and let them fall to the floor.

Rick was naked now, and Jeff opened his legs and moved between them. He caressed Rick's upper thighs and then looked at his face. "Oh, Jeff," Rick said, not knowing if it were guilt or betrayal he was feeling. But he couldn't stop. He touched Jeff's face gently, sweetly, as if giving his unspoken permission to Jeff to have any part of him that he desired. Jeff looked down at the cock made hard from desire. A drop of the sweet nectar that was Rick's sat at the very top of the man cock that Jeff wanted so badly. It seemed to be beckoning Jeff to take it, to taste its sweetness. Jeff slid his hands underneath Rick's butt and took the offering from the top of his cock.

Rick's breaths came in short gasps as he felt and watched Jeff's luscious lips take the spongy head of his manhood between them, the same lips that just moments before had met his own with a hunger that had not yet been satisfied. Jeff had his mouth over the head of Rick's cock, taking in more with each breath, until Rick could feel those beautiful lips resting on his balls. "Oh, Jeff," he said, not knowing when he had last felt this great a pleasure. Jeff sucked harder now, with an urgency to satisfy his own hunger, and held Rick's balls in his hands.

So caught up was he in his own pleasures that Jeff had not yet realized the ecstasy of his lover. It was only when Rick's body began to move to meet the inner warmth and wetness of Jeff's mouth that Jeff realized Rick's urgent need. "Damn, Jeff, I'm almost there," he said, and thrust hard into Jeff's awaiting mouth which eagerly accepted its readiness to be taken. "Oh, baby, it's too late," Rick exclaimed, and let go hard and fast the sweet nectar that Jeff had come here to claim. He took it all, so urgent was his need to be fulfilled by the body of this beautiful stranger.

He sucked hard until the tenseness of Rick's body had gone, and then softly and sweetly until the very last drop was taken and Rick's beautiful organ of manhood was soft within the welcoming cocoon of Jeff's mouth. He kissed Rick's stomach, and then looked at him.

Jeff didn't know what to say to this nice man who had been kinder to him than his own family had been, so he said, "thank you."

Rick stroked Jeff's hair, and Jeff laid his head on Rick's stomach, looking at him. "You're welcome, Jeff, but don't you think I should be thanking you?" He smiled, and Jeff managed a partial smile.

"I have to go now, Rick, but I will be back tomorrow night," Jeff said, suddenly sitting up.

"Uh, are you sure?" Rick asked, just barely getting a feel of the half hard cock inside Jeff's dress pants.

"I'm sure. I'll be back tomorrow." Jeff unlocked the door, and was gone.

Rick got up and locked the door behind Jeff. He flopped down on the bed. "What was that about?" he wondered. "Sure was what I needed, at any rate." He picked his jeans up off the floor and put them back on. Then he poured himself another drink.

Rick picked up the day's copy of the Times-Picayune and read more about the unfortunate accident of Pierre Moran. "It is most unfortunate for our family. We all loved Pierre very much. We appreciate the support from the community for our daughter, Cheri, in her loss." This from the man who had his own daughter's husband taken out. Wow! Rick went to bed early that night.

The next morning Rick awoke around nine. "Oh, man, I must not have set the alarm," he said, disgusted. He hurried and set up his equipment by the window. He was just in time to see Lucian's arrival at the warehouse. He was talking on his phone and laughing. "What a piece of work," Rick said aloud. "To Lucian, the death of someone who had somehow gotten in his way was a celebration, even if he hurt his own daughter in the process."

Rick didn't see Jeff's car yet, but about twenty minutes later he pulled up and walked slowly to the building. He looks so tired and a little lost, Rick thought. Maybe he will talk more tonight, not that I minded what he did last night.

Rick didn't see much going on at Giaconi Furniture that day. Seemed like business as usual. Around six, he watched as Jeff came out of the warehouse and got into his car. Lucian's car was still there. Rick quickly locked up his equipment since he didn't know what time Jeff would show up. Rick had gotten today's Times-Picayune, the New Orleans daily newspaper, which detailed yesterday's funeral. He placed it on the bed, opened to the page that detailed yesterday's funeral. Rick had recorded all the names and relationships, if given, of everyone the paper had listed, and sent them in an e-mail to his boss. He titled it the "Who's Who of New Orleans Underworld."

At seven, Rick heard a soft tap at the door. He unlocked it and peeked outside. He opened the door without saying a word, and locked it behind Jeff.

"I brought dinner," he said, holding up a bag of some of his favorite New Orleans cuisine. As much as he wanted to leave his family, he would miss the great food he had grown up on, he had to admit.

Rick took the bag from him and laid it out on the small table in the corner. "We'll have a buffet," he said, and looked back at Jeff.

Jeff was sitting on the bed looking at the newspaper, just like Rick had hoped he would. He wanted Jeff to talk about the family. "How was your day, Jeff?"

"Oh, it was okay," he said slowly, reading the paper as he talked. He tried not to show his emotion, but Rick had quickly realized that Jeff was not nearly as emotionless as his old man. Jeff looked troubled, maybe sad even, maybe even a little ashamed.

Rick let him read for awhile, and then asked, "Did you know the family, Jeff?"

"Oh, um, no," he lied.

"Here, let me take that from you," Rick said, and laid the paper aside.

Over dinner, Rick asked Jeff about his work. "Oh, I work at a factory."

"What kind of factory?" Rick asked.

"Giaconi Furniture. Have you heard of it?"

"No," Rick lied. "Tell me about it."

"Well, we make cedar furniture, cedar chests, and stuff like that."

Rick looked at Jeff's clothes. "You don't look like you work in a factory, Jeff."

"Oh, I um, I'm an accountant there. I don't really do the labor."

"I see," Rick said. "Been there long?"

"Yep, all my life." Jeff realized his own slip and tried to retract his words. "I mean, I started in high school working after school and on Saturdays, and then worked some while I was in college, and now I work there full-time."

"It's a family business, right? I mean, that's what the paper said," Rick commented.

"Yeah, it is," Jeff said, keeping his eyes on his food.

"It's too bad about the man's son-in-law. The family must be torn up." Rick's comment got to Jeff. He could see it in the young man's face.

They finished eating in silence, but Jeff still felt uneasy about Rick's comment. Did he know? Jeff wondered. Jeff had wanted Rick again tonight, but he felt the walls closing in on him. "Hey, Rick, I just remembered that I needed to do something tonight. Maybe we can do something later in the week."

Jeff got up and started toward the door, but Rick met him and put his arm around him, preventing him from opening the door. "Don't go, Jeff. It doesn't have to be this way. You are Jeff Giaconi, aren't you? You are the son of the very often elusive, very ruthless Lucian Giaconi, right?"

Jeff's heart started beating wildly and he could feel the acid churning in his stomach. He felt dizzy again. He started sweating. "Come here, Jeff," Rick said, and led the uncomfortable man to the bed. He wiped Jeff's face with a wet cloth. Jeff said nothing.

Once he was feeling better, though, he insisted on leaving. "I really have to go, Rick. I'm sorry."

Rick didn't stop him, though he hated to see him go. He had no idea what the man had been through, but could imagine at least some of it. The paranoia alone would be exhausting.

"Jeff?" Rick asked, just as Jeff was beginning to turn the doorknob.

"I'm sorry. I didn't mean to pry or accuse."

Jeff just nodded, and walked out the door.

Rick could hear his hurried footsteps in the hall as they became softer and softer, and then he heard nothing.

Rick sat on the bed. My God, what have I done? I'll be dead before morning. He read the rest of the day's Times-Picayune, wishing he hadn't said anything to Jeff about his family this soon. He liked Jeff, and he would do anything now to get him out of here. He obviously wants out. He has tried several times to leave, but the punishment each time had been swift and severe. Rick just wondered how many people were actually in charge of keeping an eye on Jeff.

Rick called his boss. "Well, Bill, what do you think? Kinda got close to the kid, but I think he's being watched." Rick definitely was not going to tell his boss that he really liked Jeff, or that he had gotten one of the best blowjobs of his life from him. Bill knew that Rick was gay, but he certainly didn't expect Rick to have sex in order to do his job. That's a perk, Rick said to himself.

"Well, hang low for a few days. Keep an eye on the daily paper. Maybe it will give some hint of recreational activities of the family."

Rick heard Bill chuckle on the other end of the line. Who knew what this family did for fun?

The next day, Rick ventured outside the hotel to do some sightseeing in the Big Easy. The city had always been known for its gambling and when there was a crackdown or new state limitations, they took their gambling offshore. Rick couldn't believe the number of "floating casinos" conveniently located in the Gulf of Mexico. They had even put a couple in Lake Ponchartrain. With the Gulf, the Lake, and the swamps, the Giaconi family had plenty of choices for disposing of bodies.

Rick took the trolley for much of his sightseeing, but he couldn't resist the temptation to stop in at some of the unique shops he had heard about. He walked into a bakery and didn't think he could ever leave. "Oh, I could stay here forever," he said to the lady at the counter.

"It's good eatin'," she said.

"Well, what should I try?" Rick asked the nice lady.

"Tell ya what, let me fix ya a nice sampler plate. You sit down there and I'll get ya a nice glass of sweet tea."

Rick liked the southern hospitality. He couldn't deny it. The woman brought him the sweetest tea he had ever tasted, half sugar, have tea, and a platter full of the yummiest sweet bakery treats Rick had ever tasted. "Mm, the famous New Orleans beignets," he said.

"That's right," the lady said, grinning.

Rick knew that if he finished all of the sweet treats on the entire platter, he would probably be sick, but they were all so good he had to at least try everything. He thanked the lady and tipped her very well, and she surprised him by giving him a bag of beignets to take with him. Everything he had heard about the square shaped deep fried doughy delights was true. They were scrumptious. The sweet dough was deep fried until light and airy and a golden brown color and then dipped in powdered confectioner's sugar or white sugar and cinnamon, and Rick loved them.

Rick went back to the hotel at around three in the afternoon and read the day's paper. There wasn't much in it, but he read it twice to try to find some clue of some outside interests of the Giaconi clan. He had almost given up when something caught his eye. "High stakes card tourney this weekend. Come and see how the high rollers do it."

Rick closed the paper. "Perfect. There is no way Lucian would miss that. This will probably bring other families down here, too." Rick called his boss.

"Hey, sounds great, Rick. Need some help?"

"No, but thanks. It will be easy to blend in this weekend. The Big Easy will be thick with tourists." Rick hung up the phone, showered, and went to bed.

The next morning, he set up his equipment and watched for Lucian and Jeff to show up at the warehouse, but he wasn't really counting on them being there today. They were no doubt drinking and gambling already, and it was only ten in the morning.

Rick locked up his equipment at around eleven, having seen neither Jeff's nor Lucian's cars at the warehouse. He put on his dark suit and glasses, placed his magnum in its holster, well hidden, and headed for the docks.

The entire city was packed with players and tourists and they were all crowding onto the floating casinos. If Rick didn't know who was really running the show down here in the Big

Easy, he would have been impressed. To the untrained eye, this was an impressive sight. The drinks flowed freely, the money supply was never ending, and the hostesses were practically naked. The high rollers were easy to spot. A little too obvious, Rick thought. They wore the same black suits, the same dark glasses, and had the same bodyguards they had had at the funeral. Rick did notice that the various groups, or families, seemed to keep to themselves.

He noticed one very prominent group as he walked around. The men in this group were speaking Italian, not a word of English among them. Damn, too bad I'm not writing a paper for school. This would make a great study. Rick almost laughed at himself. But to the players, this was no laughing matter. It was only a matter of time until someone got shorted or someone cheated someone, and then all hell would break loose.

Rick looked around, trying to find Jeff. He didn't want to be obvious, but he did want to talk to him. He got himself a drink, no alcohol, which surprised the man at the bar, but Rick wanted to be sober today.

From what he could see as he looked around him, he looked just like any one of them in his black suit and holstered weapon. These floating casinos are bigger than I thought. Rick looked around as best he could without being obvious. There was definitely no lack of bodyguards.

Okay, here we go, he said to himself, when he saw a very loud voiced Lucian Giaconi walk by, escorted by two very large, very mean looking bodyguards. Cigar in one hand and drink in the other, Lucian was soon also surrounded by several "working girls." What a prick, Rick thought, as he watched the ruthless Lucian leisurely run his hands up and down the girls wherever and however he chose. The wife can't do or say a thing about it, either, Rick thought.

Not far behind Lucian was Jeff, closely accompanied by Sammy and Jojo. They must be his "watchers", but Rick was not sure if they were his actual bodyguards. Jeff looked pained, and he looked tired.

Rick kept his head down, but not far enough that he could not continue to watch the two Giaconi men as they were seated. There were other men with them that Rick was pretty sure were what the members of organized crime referred to as "made men", men who had proven themselves by murdering someone, officially making them a member of the family. Sure makes college hazing seem tame, Rick almost laughed at the thought. If only these guys knew how they appeared to the real world. Their fake power was a joke. These guys were a joke. They lived in their own little world. For men who craved respect, they had no clue how to achieve it. Rick couldn't wait to get back to the real world, but he was determined more than ever now to take Jeff with him and away from all of his pain.

Rick followed the group and watched them from a safe distance. Jeff's back was to him, and Rick kept his head down. Lucian was loud, though. There was no mistaking that loud, sinister voice. The more Lucian drank, the louder he became, and the more he talked. Feeling safe and free to talk while surrounded by his bodyguards and fellow family members, Lucian talked freely. "Yeah, barely got through the funeral without losing it this time. Too bad for my girl. I'll buy her somethin' real nice with my take this weekend."

Rick noticed that no one asked Lucian about the incident. Lucian did all of the talking. "Kid was gettin' too good, thought he was better than the old man, forgot his place in the family, so I did what I had to do. I take care of this family."

So, it was true, thought Rick. He had just heard it straight from the horse's mouth and the micro recorder safely buttoned into his jacket pocket had heard it too.

Rick continued to watch the cards on the table, but stepped back a couple of steps. He did think that Lucian was getting almost too loud now. There were a lot of people here who could be listening and recording.

"They never find the body when it's my people taking care of them, right fellas?" They all agreed with Lucian, of course. "They couldn't be farther off the mark this time. Ol' Pierre is at the bottom of the Muddy Moe off the Pauline Street Wharf." Lucian laughed so hard at his own last remark that he almost choked on his drink.

Rick watched as another group of darkly clad men stepped up to the table. He noticed that Lucian immediately clammed up, too. Too bad, thought Rick. Maybe if someone heard his confessions, they would turn him in. Rick somehow doubted it, though. He was getting a good feel for just how extremely powerful Lucian Giaconi really was. I'll have to remember that, he thought.

Rick almost jumped out of his skin when a man came up behind him. "Sorry, buddy. Just wanted to offer you another drink." "No, thanks," Rick replied, knowing not to accept a drink from someone he didn't know or from someone who didn't look like he worked here. Damn, I hope they're not onto me. Shit, now I'm as paranoid as the rest of them. I really do fit in here.

Rick looked over and noticed that Jeff was no longer seated at the table. He looked around. Sammy and JoJo were still here, but they were no longer attached to Jeff like they had been. "I wonder if they've even noticed that Jeff is gone." The two men seemed to be talking about something and had completely ignored the table.

Rick walked away from the table and wandered throughout the casino, but saw no sign of Jeff. He didn't think Jeff would be brave enough, or stupid enough rather, to try to leave again.

Rick eventually walked back into the room where Lucian was still seated. The casino was so crowded with tourists and other gamblers that he could barely walk around. The table was surrounded, and so was Lucian. Rick still did not see Jeff, and Sammy and JoJo were getting cozy with a couple of "hostesses." Rick decided to leave. He didn't think Lucian would say anything more about the business with members of opposing families so close by, or at least who Rick thought were members of opposing families.

Rick took a cab back to his hotel. He hadn't realized how hot he had gotten until he walked into the much less crowded air conditioned hotel. He opened the door of his room and quickly locked it behind him. He looked around like he always did. You never knew who might be watching you, or who could be waiting for you. He turned on the shower and took off his clothes, locking his .22 Magnum in the drawer.

The shower felt good. Rick was not accustomed to the heat and humidity that held this city captive. He tilted his head up and let the water hit his face. He let the water push his hair back and he closed his eyes as the water continued to hit his face. He was so relaxed that he thought he could fall asleep standing up in the shower.

Suddenly and without warning, Rick felt his body being held and backed up to the back wall of the shower. His eyes flew open and he started to speak. "Wha...?"

"Shh, it's okay. Don't talk. Just listen."

It was Jeff, and he had his hand covering Rick's mouth so that he couldn't scream. "Don't scream, okay? Just listen to me. You promise?"

Rick nodded. Jeff took his hand off of Rick's mouth.

"What are you doing here and how did you get in?" Rick whispered.

"I lied to the hotel clerk and said that I was with you."

"Don't they know who you are?"

"I don't think so," Jeff hoped. "I can't be sure, though."

Once Rick had gotten over the shock of Jeff being in the shower with him, he noticed that Jeff was naked. Jeff pressed his wet naked body against Rick's. "Hold me, Rick," he commanded. Jeff searched for Rick's mouth through the steam of the shower and kissed him with the same urgency that he had the night he had ravished Rick. Jeff pinned Rick's head against the wall of the shower and kissed him, forcing his mouth open.

Jeff's free hand slid down Rick's back and onto his butt. He pulled it open, and the water felt good hitting hard in that sensitive space where the two halves parted. Jeff brought his hand around, forcing it between Rick's legs. "I need you," he said, and Rick opened his legs for Jeff. He stroked Rick beneath his balls, watching for his reaction. Jeff heard him moan through the noise of the rushing water. Jeff held Rick's balls, pulling them downward, squeezing them almost too hard, and then holding Rick's cock that was now hard.

Jeff stroked Rick's hardness, forced his lips off of Rick's, and looked at him. "Touch me, Rick," he commanded. Rick reached for Jeff's cock and could feel it rise to its fullness in his hand. Jeff forced Rick's hand down to his balls and formed his hand around them. Jeff moaned under Rick's touch. "Do you want me, Rick?" "Yes," he said.

They kissed again, and stroked each other's hard cock, the water mixing with their pre-cum now oozing from its recent escape. Jeff's fingers were eager to be inside Rick, but that would have to wait. Jeff knew they hadn't much time. "We haven't much time, Rick. I need you now." Rick held Jeff's cock and began to bring him closer to orgasm. Jeff was pumping Rick's cock hard and fast. "Don't stop, Rick. Don't stop for anything." Jeff kissed Rick as he pumped harder. Rick could barely breathe and his knees felt weak as Jeff brought him to climax. Jeff encouraged him to keep pumping his cock harder and faster, and he laid his lead against Rick's chest as he emptied his heavy balls onto Rick's hand. He watched as the cum drifted down Rick's leg, mixing with the water of the shower, and drifted into the drain.

He held Rick close to him and looked up at him and kissed him. "Hurry, Rick, we have to go," Jeff urged, and soaped his hands and then Rick's and his bodies. Rick wanted to ask where they had to go but waited for Jeff's answer to that, whenever it would come. Jeff rinsed them both, and then urged Rick to dry himself and dress quickly.

Once out of the shower, Rick asked, "Jeff, where do we need to go?"

"I am leaving again, Rick. You are the only one who can help me. Take me with you back to your home. I don't care where it is. I will go anywhere with you, but they will be looking for me soon. I saw you at the casino today. I know you care."

Rick was so shocked and so concentrated on dressing himself that he barely had time to ask or answer any questions. "So you are?"

"Yes, Rick, I am Jeff Giaconi, the son and assumed Underboss to the man you spoke of, Lucian Giaconi. But I cannot stay. I will die here. I would rather die than live this way."

Rick understood, but Jeff had no idea who *he* was, a Federal Agent. He couldn't hand Jeff over to the authorities. He *was* the authorities. If he did turn him in, Jeff would die within days, if not hours, at the hands of his own people.

Jeff hurried to help Rick pack. "I have a taxi waiting downstairs," he said with urgency.

"Here, take my trunk, and I'll get the rest of my stuff," Rick instructed.

Rick didn't want Jeff to see his weapon and would pack this once Jeff was gone. Rick knew that he had to go because even in the crowds that this weekend had brought to the city, someone surely would have seen Jeff leave the casino, and someone surely would have seen Jeff come here. Rick knew that he was in just as much danger now that Jeff was.

Jeff took the locked cabinet and put it in the taxi. As soon as he was gone, Rick tucked his .22 Magnum mini in its holster and threw everything else into the two large suitcases he had brought. One big satchel thrown over his shoulder and Rick was ready to go.

Jeff was back and he helped Rick with his suitcases. "I have to check out, Jeff," he said.

"Hurry, Rick, please," Jeff pleaded.

The lobby was crowded and anyone could be watching him, or them. Checkout went fast, and Jeff slouched down in the taxi. "Airport, please," Rick said to the driver. Jeff did not look at Rick the entire time, and Rick knew that was wise. The driver could easily be persuaded to talk.

Jeff paid the driver when they arrived at Louis Armstrong International Airport, and they hurried inside. "Rick, where are we going? We have no tickets."

"Well, as far as we know, no one knows me. We'll go to my home."

"Okay," Jeff agreed, still not knowing where Rick called home.

"Wait, we're not going to Kansas City, are we?" Jeff asked.

"No. Home is Denver, Colorado."

They were fortunate not to have to wait long to get a flight, and even more fortunate that it was a direct flight. Jeff looked around the plane. There weren't that many passengers on board. More were coming into the city this weekend than were leaving. Jeff looked around him again. "Relax," Rick whispered. "I can help you."

Jeff thought the world of this nice man and felt a strong connection to him, just as Rick felt for Jeff. Rick wondered what Jeff would think of him when he discovered that he was a federal agent.

When Jeff was satisfied that he was safe, at least for now, he reclined his seat and closed his eyes. His head soon fell onto Rick's arm, and Rick felt that same sense of sadness for Jeff that he had in New Orleans. He just now realized that Jeff had brought nothing with him. He had no clothes, no anything, not even a toothbrush. He really does want out, he thought.

When the pilot announced their arrival in Denver, Jeff sat straight up. He had been dreaming and thought someone was talking to him. "We're here, Jeff, in Denver," Rick told him.

Jeff felt that all too familiar fear of what might be waiting for him on the ground. "Do you think they're waiting for me, Rick?"

"I doubt it, Jeff. But here, put my sweatshirt on with the hood up. It will be a lot cooler here, anyway. I think they said it was around fifty degrees."

"Fifty degrees? That's so cold!"

"No, Jeff, it's just right," Rick assured him.

Jeff put the sweatshirt on and awaited his fate.

When he and Rick walked into the terminal, there was no one waiting for him, no one that he could see anyway. Jeff kept the sweatshirt hood up until they were on their way to Rick's house. Rick had taken his own car to the airport instead of one of the agency vehicles, and now he was relieved that he had. Imagine what Jeff would have done if he had seen an agency car waiting for him.

"It is *cold* here," Jeff remarked. "I do like the snow, though. I've only seen snow a couple of times, at my grandparents' home in Kansas when I was a young boy."

Rick looked over at him for a second. "You have family in Kansas?"

"Yeah, my mom is from Kansas. She met Dad when he was stationed at Fort Riley."

Rick was more than curious now. "Did she know, Jeff, what she was getting into?"

"No, she didn't. She went to New Orleans only a couple of times before they were married and of course, Dad was very careful to let Mom see only what he wanted her to see. I think they pretty much just stayed with his parents."

"That's interesting, Jeff. I just assumed that she was in the know, so to speak."

It was quite a drive to Rick's house, and since Jeff was talking, Rick wasn't going to stop him. "Where was the wedding, your Mom's and Dad's? The place must have been flooded with your dad's people."

"That was another of Dad's very carefully calculated moves. The wedding was in Kansas City where my mom was living with her parents. Very few of Dad's people made the trip north."

"So, your mother's ancestry is what, then?"

"I'm not sure exactly, British probably. They're a pretty waspy bunch."

Rick looked confused. "Waspy?"

"You know, waspy. I think it means White, Anglo-Saxon (English speaking), Protestant. I think it's used mainly to describe the early settlers, you know, in the original colonies."

Rick was learning more and more about the Giaconi family. "Lucian had brought someone new into the family," he said to himself. "Your dad's family didn't mind that your mother was not Italian?"

"Didn't seem to, but no one talks, no one. I really didn't understand it myself fully until I was in my teens. Italians were just another of the groups that added to the diversity of New Orleans."

Rick pulled into his driveway and wondered what Jeff must think of his small home. "Not like the old homestead down south, huh?"

"It's beautiful, Rick, just like its owner."

Rick couldn't believe that he was beginning to blush in front of Jeff, but he was.

Rick parked his car outside in the driveway, because he didn't want Jeff to see the U.S. Government tag on the car sitting in the garage. Jeff looked around nervously. What a life, thought Rick. He unlocked the door and let Jeff go in ahead of him. Rick brought his suitcases in, but left the locked cabinet in the trunk of his car.

"Could you help me carry these down the hall?" he asked Jeff.

Jeff carried the bags to the far bedroom, and once he was out of sight Rick placed his gun in a drawer in the kitchen.

"I'll let you pick out some clothes, Jeff. Choose whatever you like. Most of mine should fit you."

"Thanks, Rick," he said, and changed into some loose fitting sweats.

They were both tired from the flight, and Rick never kept much food in the house since he was hardly ever home. "Hungry, Jeff?"

"Not really."

"Well, you were sleeping when they brought our meals on the plane. You sure you're not hungry?"

"I'm sure, Rick. Thanks."

"Well, I'm going to have some wine," Rick announced, and headed straight for the bar. He poured a glass for himself and then handed one to Jeff.

"I missed this more than anything, almost," he admitted. Jeff loved Rick's wine. "It's like Sweet Tea, with a kick to it."

Rick laughed. "I can honestly say I've never had it described that way."

Whatever it was that was so strong between them was quickly bubbling to the surface once again. Rick set his glass down, and Jeff quickly set his down too, and helped himself to a serving of Rick. He straddled Rick and settled in his lap. He held his face in his hands, leaned up, pressed his body against Rick's, and tasted his lips. He licked the wine that lingered there, holding Rick's face, forming Rick's mouth to meet his lips. Rick's arms were around Jeff, holding him close, welcoming his lips. "Rick," he said, but said nothing more. He bent Rick's head back on the sofa, and kissed him harder. Their tongues met and danced inside both of their mouths.

Jeff pulled Rick's shirt up and searched his chest for the buds of desire and teased them to their fullest hardness. Rick's hands opened the sweatpants that were loose on Jeff. "Mm," he moaned, as he held Jeff's ass in his hands. With Jeff's legs on either side of Rick's, his butt cheeks were separated, and Rick eagerly slid his fingertips along the open crevice. Jeff gasped, and stopped kissing for just a second, resting his lips on Rick's. "Don't stop," he whispered. Rick slid his fingertips downward until he found Jeff's eager entrance. He circled it with his fingers, and then let just a fingertip enter.

Jeff pulled the sweatpants down, and his full erect cock sprang forward. "Whoa, something hit me," Rick joked.

"Something you can't refuse," Jeff assured him.

"Got that right," Rick agreed, and grasped it in one hand, and slid his hand upward along the length of it. "You are one hot man, Jeff."

Jeff had never been turned on by anyone like he was by Rick. "Take me, Rick. Take all of me." Jeff's mouth was on Rick's ear as he spoke.

In one sudden movement, Rick lifted Jeff up by his naked ass and carried him down the hall and dropped him on the bed which sloshed underneath him. "What is this, a waterbed?"

"I just can't part with it," Rick teased. He stripped Jeff of the old sweats he was wearing and tossed them on the floor. Jeff pulled his shirt over his head, and he lay there with his arms spread, his legs spread, offering his entire self to Rick.

Rick did a pseudo-striptease for Jeff and waved his hard cock at him. "Proud of that?"

"You know it, babe. You know you want it."

Jeff licked his lips in response. Rick got onto the bed and slowly opened Jeff's legs so that he could have what he wanted. He licked Jeff's inner thighs, coming to where his leg met his groin, and then after he had licked his way up on both sides, he slid his tongue underneath each of Jeff's large balls. "Mm, I like these," Rick said, as he scooped each one into his mouth and rolled it around with his tongue. He slid the tip of his tongue onto the velvety space below Jeff's balls until he reached the parting of his butt cheeks. Jeff gasped and moaned under Rick's touch, his cock now a leaky faucet of pre-cum.

Rick was a good lover, especially when he was with someone he loved, and he loved Jeff. His hands were underneath Jeff, enjoying his gorgeous ass, searching for the glorious pleasure entrance that had caused the gasps and moans from Jeff earlier. A fingertip entered, and Jeff gasped again. Rick held it there, and kissed his way up Jeff's cock, making loud kissing noises all the way to the top. "Mm, are these for me?" "Ohhh," Jeff responded, and Rick sucked the drops from the purple head, and licked the ones that had gotten away off of Jeff's stomach. "Damn, Rick." Jeff's eyes were closed, and his body was tensing with anticipation. Rick held the head of Jeff's cock between his lips and slowly sucked his way to the base, taking all of Jeff's beautiful cock into the warmth of his mouth. Jeff had plenty to offer Rick, and Rick devoured all of it. He could feel Jeff's tenseness, and sucked harder, with slow steady movements from the base to the top of Jeff's manhood.

Jeff was grasping the bed to hold on as long as he could. Rick had wanted Jeff from that first night when him had come to his room, and he didn't want it to end. He began to slow his pace, but Jeff urged him to go faster. "Don't make me wait," he urged. As much as Rick would have wanted to make this last, he cared too much for Jeff to not give him what he wanted. He sucked harder and entered Jeff a little more. Jeff thrust his hardness as far into Rick's mouth as he could, feeding his own need and also that of Rick to have him in this way. "Oh, shit, Rick," he said, as Rick brought him very close to orgasm. Jeff could feel his large heavy balls emptying, and he pulled Rick's head up and off of his cock and onto his lips. Rick grabbed Jeff's cock and felt it emptying between their bodies.

Surprised that Jeff had stopped him, Rick gave him a questioning look. While he tried to catch his breath, Jeff said, "Put it in me, Rick, all of it." Rick scooped up the cum and massaged Jeff's crack with it, and then slid it inside. "Get it all, Rick," he urged. Rick got as much as he could and swept it just inside Jeff's opening. "All the way in, Rick." Rick didn't realize Jeff's urgency. Jeff was starved for love.

Jeff scooted out from under Rick and turned onto his stomach. He pulled his legs up under him and spread them for Rick. "Go in deep, Rick. Fuck me." Okay, now Rick knew just what Jeff wanted. Rick swirled the cum deep inside Jeff, and Jeff jumped when he touched the place that he was begging for him to touch. "Oh, yeah, Rick, that's it. Now, use your dick." Rick kissed each of Jeff's butt cheeks lightly and then placed his cock head at Jeff's entrance and pushed it in. Jeff gasped.

Rick was pretty sure this was Jeff's first time, but it was what he had wanted. "Don't stop now, Rick." Rick pushed slowly into Jeff, holding onto his thighs the entire time. Rick thought his head was going to explode. "I'm going to lose it if I'm not careful," he thought. Jeff definitely hadn't been entered before, and the feeling of his tightness was more than just a little bit of a turn-on. Jeff jumped again when Rick hit the mark again and again. "That's it, ooh, that's good, Rick." Rick knew he wasn't going to last long. "Jeff, I'm almost there," he warned.

Jeff pushed back against Rick, a definite sign that Rick was not to pull out. Rick caressed Jeff's butt and then reached underneath him and grasped his cock which was half hard now. "Just hold it, Rick." Rick held Jeff's cock firmly in his hands and with just a couple more hard thrusts he fell onto Jeff as his cum filled Jeff deep inside. Jeff had a second orgasm while Rick was holding his cock. Damn, the kid was horny, he said to himself. "Ohh, that's it, Rick. Damn, that was, oh, damn."

Jeff lay flat on the bed underneath Rick. "Don't leave, Rick. Stay on top of me." Rick lay on the bed on Jeff's back, their hearts beating fast and both of them trying to catch their breath.

Jeff was not as tired as Rick, and he wanted to talk. "Stay there, Rick. Tell me why you were alone in New Orleans."

"Oh, I really don't have anyone in my life, Jeff."

"Now you do," he said. "Yes, Jeff, now I do."

Rick kissed Jeff's shoulder, and his soft dick slithered out of Jeff. "Face me, Jeff."

Jeff turned onto his side and faced Rick. Rick pulled the covers up over both of them. Jeff was not used to the cooler temperatures that Rick preferred. Rick liked having someone in his bed, someone who would be there in the morning. "Do you see your grandparents often?"

"The ones in Kansas, no. Grandpa died and Grandma lives alone. We never did see them much, even as kids. I learned as I got older that Dad couldn't take the chance of having someone find out about him. He didn't want any trouble with the Kansas City families."

"Did he know any of them?"

"Not really. He tried not to. Mom had a cousin who lived close to the Nebraska line and Dad thought that the guy began to suspect about the family. He started asking questions about where the money came from because there was no way we could be living the way we were with just a small furniture store. He was right about that, too, and Dad knew that he had to get rid of him."

Rick had no idea the scope of the Giaconi operation. "How did he do it, Jeff?"

"I'm not sure how he did it, but he somehow got some sort of poison into him. I think maybe my grandparents gave it to the man, not knowing that it was poison. Anyway, it made him sick, and when they operated on him, it showed up as cancer. But it was not cancer. It was a 'special delivery' from his first cousin's husband. The man died, too, and left two daughters who were then just barely out of their teens, and a young widow."

Rick looked at Jeff. He loved him, but he also wondered what types of crimes were in Jeff's past. "So, the autopsy didn't show anything?"

"Oh, there was no autopsy. Dad convinced Mom to beg the widow not to do that. The man's widow was so distraught that she just wanted to let her dead husband lie in peace."

Wow, what a mess, Rick thought. Jeff continued his story. "What was worse, they made the man's widow feel really bad and told her and everyone else they knew that if she had taken better care of her husband somehow, he never would have gotten sick and died. That's how sick my so-called family is, and that's why I had to leave."

Rick stroked Jeff's arm. "Let's get some sleep, Jeff." Jeff's eyes were closing as he talked and soon he was breathing loudly and sleeping soundly. Rick was asleep within minutes and didn't wake up until six the next morning.

It was still dark and Jeff was still sleeping, so he quietly got out of bed and took his cell phone into the garage to contact his boss.

"Where have you been, Rick? I've been trying to reach you."

"I had to turn my phone off, Bill. I'm back in Denver. They were getting too close."

"Okay, good thinking, Rick. Always go with your instincts. Get anything on the kid?"

"Some information. Lucian married a girl from Kansas. She had no idea she was married to the mob, until it was too late. Guess the kids didn't know until they were in their teens."

Bill was silent for a few minutes. "Think I'll go down there, Rick. I'll stay in a different hotel than the one you stayed in, and ask around."

"Watch yourself, Bill. It's worse than we thought."

Rick tucked his phone back inside his pocket and went back inside the house. Jeff had just gotten up and was walking down the hall toward him. "What are you doing?"

"Oh, I needed to make a call, and the reception is better in the garage," he lied, realizing how close he had come to being found out. What if Jeff had opened the door to the garage?

Rick started the coffee, and Jeff walked over to the sliding door off of the dining room. "Wow, Rick. This is beautiful."

B.K. Wright   149

"I assume you're talking about the sunrise and the mountains."

"Definitely. Look at this."

"I see it every day, Jeff. It is beautiful."

"And to think, I live in a swamp."

"It's not a swamp, Jeff, although it is a little too hot and humid for my taste."

"Mind if I turn on the news?"

"Help yourself, Jeff."

There was breaking news from New Orleans. Jeff had to sit down to keep from falling. "It appears that the Underboss of the Giaconi family, Jeff, has been missing for two days. The known gangster was last seen entering the Bayou Hotel, but there has been no trace of him since."

Rick sighed in relief. He had used an alias at the airport, so he had hoped that was where his trail ended.

The reporter continued. "The witness indicated that she did not see Jeff leave the hotel, but upon a thorough search of every room, there has been no sign of the mafia second-in-command."

"They called me a gangster, Rick. That's not me. That's my dad."

"I know, Jeff. I know." Rick understood a lot more than he had when he first arrived in New Orleans. "So, you think your dad had the place searched."

"Hell, yes, Rick. He probably went to the airport, too."

"Don't worry, Jeff. I used an alias."

"But our descriptions, Rick, what about them?"

"Let's just hope that no one at the airport saw which flight we took."

Rick was nervous now. It only took one person. They waited through a commercial to hear the rest. "I thought they were coming back with more, Jeff."

"I'm sure they were, Rick, but Dad probably shut them up."

"So, tell me about the guy in Kansas, Jeff."

"Oh, that's really all I know. I don't even know where his daughters are now. They would be about my age, I think."

Rick thought about this. I could try to contact them, but from what Jeff has said they wouldn't know any more than he has already told me, he said to himself.

"Mind if I look for more news?"

"Help yourself, Jeff. The remote is on the table."

Rick was thinking about all of this. "It doesn't sound like there is much of a Kansas connection any longer. Seems like Lucian kept his cards pretty close to the vest, at least as far as business was concerned."

The phone rang, and Rick jumped. He picked it up. "Rick, you weren't kidding, man. I checked in downtown at a small hotel, but I hadn't been here an hour before I overhead some men talking in the bakery connected to the hotel. I'm pretty sure they were part of the operation. I could barely hear them, but from what I could gather, they think that Jeff either ran away again or he was taken by one of the other families from one of the casinos. They aren't too happy with Jeff's bodyguards, that's for sure."

"Hmm," Rick said, not wanting to give himself away to Jeff. "Which way is it headed?"

"Can't say, Rick. I think they're looking at the other families, and a possible abduction," Bill informed him.

Rick was thinking that would be ideal for Jeff, at least for awhile. Things were bound to get ugly when the other families discovered that it had all been a setup. Then Jeff would be a wanted man for sure. "Well, what do you have planned for the week?"

"I don't know, Rick. Think I'd better hang low. May check out the casinos."

"Well, be careful," Rick said.

"Sure thing," his boss said, and hung up.

Jeff had found another news channel so he had not heard Rick's words, though Rick hadn't said anything that would give himself away. "Do you have to go to work today, Rick?"

"No, I have a couple of weeks off."

"Oh, yeah, guess I cut your vacation short," Jeff said apologetically.

Rick walked over to him and kissed his lips. "You are the best part of my vacation."

Rick sat with him and watched the news. They weren't saying anything more, just the same thing they had already said. Rick wanted to tell Jeff everything. He couldn't believe that one of the men he was trying to put behind bars was sitting right here in his living room. If he could somehow get him to cooperate with the FBI, or "turn state's evidence", as the old saying went. I never intended on falling in love with the enemy, he told himself. Then he remembered his grandmother's old saying, "The road to hell is paved with good intentions." If something happens to Bill in New Orleans, I will just die, he thought.

"Hey, Rick, where did you go?" Jeff asked. "I've been talking to you for several minutes."

"Oh, guess I'm just tired," Rick said, and he *was* tired, and confused.

"What line of work are you in, Rick. I can't believe that I've never asked you that."

"I do some consulting, Jeff, securities, bonds, things of that nature."

Jeff didn't ask anything more, and Rick was glad, because he was almost sick from covering up, at least with Jeff.

Rick's cell phone rang, and it was Bill. "Excuse me, Jeff. I need to take this. I'll be in the garage for better reception."

Jeff nodded.

Rick went into the garage, closing the door behind him. He sat on the step and talked to his boss.

"Okay, Rick. I went to the casino, and man, things are heating up. Everyone is suspect, and there are members of more than just a couple of the families here. If we can find Jeff before the family does, we can get everybody. I'm going back there, but I'll be calling you on your cell phone from now on. Can't take the chance that this place might be bugged."

"Sounds good, Bill. Keep in touch."

Bill tucked his phone into his pocket and then turned to walk back inside, but was not prepared for what he saw.

"Jeff."

"That's right. You know who *I* am. Who the fuck are *you*?"

"Jeff, it's not what you think."

Jeff pushed Rick out of the way and walked over to the car in the garage. "Thought there wasn't room in here for your car. Well, this is a two car garage and there is only one car in here. What gives?"

Rick followed Jeff as he walked to the back of the car. Jeff kicked the license plate that clearly read U.S. Government, making a dent in the middle of the metal. Fear and hatred filled him as he stared at Rick. "You set me up, you bastard. You took advantage of me and my situation." He lunged at Rick, but Rick moved. Jeff caught himself on the steps. "You bastard, Rick, if that *is* your real name. Well, I guess you win. Bet your boss had a good laugh when you told him you were fucking the man you were sent to bring back to him. Well, you really got me, didn't you? You had me right where you wanted me. You had me in your bed."

Jeff stood up, but Rick was ready for him. He stood back and waited to see what he would do, but he knew that he could take Jeff down if he had to. He certainly had enough training. Jeff had scraped his chin on the step and was holding it.

"Are you hurt?" Rick asked.

"Oh, what the fuck do you care?" Jeff lunged at him again. He was strong and he pushed Rick backward, almost pushing him against the car. Rick caught himself and was able to hold Jeff's arms behind his back.

"Let go of me, you bastard," he screamed.

Rick was not as big as Jeff, but he was stronger. "You listen to me, Jeff." Jeff's response to that was to spit in Rick's face. "Nice, Jeff, real nice."

Jeff squirmed his way free of Rick's hold and pushed him to the ground. Rick caught himself, but was thankful for the old piece of carpet on the floor of the garage that softened his fall, at least a little. Jeff was soon on top of him throwing punches, and Rick was trying to grab his arms.

"Jeff, stop it. Hear me out."

"I'm not interested in anything you might have to say, you bastard."

Once Rick was able to grab Jeff's hands, he rolled him over and then rolled on top of him. He held Jeff's arms flat on the floor over his head.

"Let me go," he snarled.

Rick had his legs over Jeff's so that he couldn't kick him. They were both breathing hard now, but Rick tried to talk to him anyway. "It's true, Jeff. I'm a federal agent and I did go to New Orleans to try to stop your dad from killing. But things changed while I was down there. Something happened to me down there."

"Get off me, you fucking liar. Don't tell me you care about me. You don't."

"You know I care, Jeff. Why would I have helped you escape if I didn't care?"

"You brought me here for leverage. Now you can get anything from my dad. You know he's looking for me."

Rick looked at Jeff and the hurt in his eyes that he had put there, and it made him sick. The kid had been hurt enough already. "Look, Jeff. I'm telling you the truth. That's why I didn't tell my boss. If I didn't care about you, I would have had him here so fast you wouldn't have known what hit you. Now he is in New Orleans and his life could be in danger at this moment. Don't you see that?"

"Shut up, and get your ass off me," Jeff shouted.

"You know you don't mean that," Rick said, and kissed Jeff's trembling lips.

Jeff moved his head to get away.

"Stop kissing me, you bastard," he yelled.

"Is that what you want, Jeff? It's not, and you know it."

Rick held Jeff's lips in his own and kissed him again. Jeff mumbled something, but stopped moving his head from side to side. He kissed Rick. He wanted Rick, but he didn't want to want Rick. He ripped his lips off of Rick's.

"Get off," he screamed.

Rick ran his lips along Jeff's lips. "You know you want me. I want you, Jeff."

"No, I do not want you. Now get off me." He lifted his head off the floor, but was met by Rick's lips. Rick kissed him. He couldn't help it. He wanted him.

"Stop it," he mumbled.

"You know you want me just as much as I want you," Rick said.

Jeff kissed Rick hard, as if he were trying to hurt him, but he still had raw sexual urges that he wanted Rick to satisfy.

Jeff had lost some of his fight from sheer exhaustion, but he continued to do the dance of kissing Rick and then forcing his lips off of Rick's. "You don't want me, huh? Are you sure?" Rick was holding Jeff's hands with one hand, and undoing his pants with the other. He forced the zipper down and pulled Jeff's hard cock out.

"Uh, stop," he mumbled.

"You don't want me to stop. I would say you want me just as much as I want you." Rick's hand stroked Jeff's hard cock and swept across the swollen head.

"That's not for you," Jeff shouted.

"You sure?"

Jeff closed his eyes and began thrusting his cock into Rick's hand.

"Fuck my hand, Jeff. You know you want it."

Rick forced Jeff's jeans down and forced his hand between Jeff's legs. Jeff bent his knees and moaned. "That's it," Rick said. Rick stroked hard beneath Jeff's balls, but didn't stop there. He forced a finger down and forced Jeff's cheeks apart until he found his hole. He thrust a finger upward with a hard thrust. "Uh," Jeff groaned, but then started fucking Rick's finger. "Yeah, that's my Jeff." Jeff couldn't help it. He wanted Rick to fuck him. He wanted Rick to suck him.

Rick had opened Jeff's shirt and sucked hard on his nipples. He moved down and took the head of Jeff's cock between his lips. He had let go of Jeff's arms, but they were still on the ground over Jeff's head. "Harder, Rick, harder," he shouted. Rick thrust two fingers deep inside of Jeff and took more of his cock into his mouth. "Ohhh," Jeff moaned, and bucked hard against Rick's fingers. "Rick, shit," he said, warning that he was going to empty his balls into Rick's mouth. He thrust his dick hard into Rick's mouth, feeling the back of his throat with the head, and he was sure he could feel his balls emptying with his climax. He came so hard that it was almost painful.

Rick continued to suck Jeff's dick from the base to the tip, pulling it with his mouth, stretching it, forcing every drop to give up its fight as if each stubborn drop were a part of Jeff that refused to surrender to the truth of his love. "Ohh," Jeff moaned, over and over, as Rick kept going until Jeff's dick was soft. It had become sensitive to Rick's hard forceful sucking, but Jeff was not willing to admit that to Rick, admit defeat, that is. He felt the need to win this time, to not allow Rick to defeat him. Both felt they had defeated the other somehow.

Jeff panted after his forceful release, and Rick forced Jeff's jeans all the way off and forced him onto his stomach. "Uh," Jeff moaned, too drained to fight. "What the fu...," he started.

"Give me that hot ass of yours. You think I don't care? You think I don't love you?" Rick ripped Jeff's shirt off and forced his legs underneath him, spread his cheeks apart, and ran his tongue along his crack. He thrust a finger deep inside and Jeff moaned. With one hand, Rick undid his own jeans and shoved them down, and then he forced Jeff's butt cheeks apart with the top of his dick and slid it between them. Then he raised Jeff's ass to him and licked him, probing him deep inside with his tongue.

"Oh, damn, Rick," Jeff said, and moaned. "Shit," he said, with every thrust of Rick's tongue at his inner pleasure.

Rick felt underneath Jeff and slid his hand along Jeff's cock, half hard again just as Rick had hoped. Rick made Jeff wetter inside than he had ever been, with the wetness of his tongue mixed with the wetness of Jeff's cum. Rick pulled his tongue out with a force that caused another "uh" from Jeff, and quickly replaced it with the head of his cock. He pushed hard against Jeff, forcing the swollen head of his penis inside, followed by the entire length of his hard cock.

"Damn, Rick," Jeff groaned.

"You want me to stop, Jeff? Hm, you want me to stop, or do you want me to fuck you? I can stop right now. Say the word."

"Fuck me, you bastard," he demanded.

Rick held onto Jeff's thighs and plunged his hard cock into Jeff's ass over and over. After several hard and unrelenting thrusts, Jeff's erection was full and hanging down from his body. Rick grabbed it and pulled hard, forcing Jeff to explode just as he filled Jeff's ass with his warm cum. Rick exploded forcefully, causing an unexpected moan from Jeff. "That's it, you like that, don't you, Jeff?" Rick thrust once more, and then pulled Jeff's legs out from under him and he lay on top of him, their chests heaving beneath them as they fought to catch their breath.

"Okay, okay, I give," Jeff panted. "You made your point."

Rick's soft dick slid out of Jeff, and he moved up to Jeff's neck. "And what point is that?" he asked, beside Jeff's ear.

"You care, okay, I get it."

"Do you, Jeff?"

"Yes," he said. "Now would you get off of me? This piece of carpet is rubbing me raw."

"You promise to be good?" Rick was half teasing now.

"I promise," Jeff replied, in a childlike voice.

Rick got up off of him, and then helped him up. Jeff had carpet marks on his front and his back. Rick squeezed his butt. "You need a shower," he said.

"Mm," he added. "I am a pretty hot piece of ass," Jeff teased. "This isn't over, Rick."

"I know." Rick had no idea where to go from here, but he knew he couldn't give up on Jeff or return him to his family or turn him in to the agency.

Rick cleaned himself up while Jeff took a shower. When he came out, he sat down and looked defiantly at Rick. "Now what?"

"I don't know, Jeff. I don't know."

"I really don't think your boss is in trouble, as long as he's smart. But if he lets it be known that he's with the Feds, he will get killed. My father won't think twice about having him taken out. I couldn't begin to count how many people our family has killed." Rick looked at him. He knew. He had been fighting organized crime for a long, long time. "And, you know I can never leave the family. I've tried. They always find me. The reminders by the family of my loyalty to them are severe."

Rick just nodded. He had heard stories about reminders, as Jeff called them. "Where did you go those other times?"

"There were two times, Rick. The first time was right after Cheri's wedding. There were a lot of people around and I made the mistake of trusting one of Pierre's friends. Pierre tipped him off, said it was a setup, and that his friend was going to make me think I was in the clear and then bring me back. Pierre was terrified of Dad. He knew all about the family. I really thought the guy was going to help me. How stupid was I?"

Rick got up and walked over to Jeff. He sat down beside him and held his hand. "You're not stupid, Jeff. You're just in a bad situation."

"Yeah, Rick, and that bad situation is called my life."

"Well, now I understand where your distrust of strangers comes from."

"You mean my distrust of family, friends, and strangers. In my world, Rick, you cannot trust anyone."

Rick thought about this. "But you trusted me, Jeff. You were willing to go anywhere with me. Why?"

Jeff looked at him. He hadn't thought about all of this. "I don't know. You seemed different, and then, there was the sex. You know how good that is."

Rick did know. The two of them definitely had that going for them. "But if I had known who you really are, I never would have gotten into your bed," he said, with that fiery hatred bubbling back up to the surface. He took his hand away from Rick's hold.

"You giving up on us, then?"

Jeff closed his eyes. He didn't answer.

"*I'm* not ready to give up on us, Jeff."

"Look, Rick, what's left for us? I mean, where do we go from here? Like I said, there is no way out, for me."

Jeff knew that Rick could walk away any time he wanted, but it was just a matter of time before he had to go back to New Orleans and the family.

"How hard are you willing to fight, Jeff?"

Jeff gave Rick an odd look. "What are you talking about? You can't fight my family, Rick."

"Well, just humor me for a few minutes here. How far would you take it, if you could?"

"I'd cooperate, if that's what you mean. Before Pierre was killed, I guess I kinda thought Dad wasn't too bad, but having Pierre killed, that was the end, and the scene at the church, pretending to be sad for Cheri, when the old man was responsible for his own daughter's grief. He didn't care. I guess I overlooked it when he had me beat up for leaving, but Pierre will never be back."

Rick needed to think. He needed to talk to Bill. His boss knew that he was gay. Hell, Bill swung both ways. He was probably in bed right now with a man *and* a woman.

"What's goin' on, Rick?"

"I just don't quite know what to do?"

Jeff laughed. "There's no way, Rick. My life was decided for me before I was born. That's the deal."

Rick pushed his hair back. Then he parked his butt on Jeff's legs and pushed him back against the sofa. "What are you doing, Rick?"

Rick's legs were outside of Jeff's, and he held Jeff's head. Rick kissed him tenderly. "Look, Jeff. I'm not willing to let you go. I want you. I need you. But mostly, I need you to believe in us. That's the only way we can be together. Do you? Do you believe in us?" Jeff had no idea that Rick was so passionate outside of sex. "Do you believe in us, Jeff?"

Jeff closed his eyes. He was tired both physically and mentally and had been for years. He opened his eyes and looked at Rick. He saw something in Rick's eyes that he hadn't seen before, or maybe he hadn't taken the time to see it before now. "Are you saying...? I mean, do you love me, Rick?"

"Yes, Jeff, oh God, yes," he said, and kissed him, passionately this time, like a lover, like he hadn't felt anything as strong as this.

Rick was kissing him with his lips, but Jeff felt as if he were being kissed by Rick's entire body. Rick forced his lips to leave Jeff's, and Jeff moaned. "I want you so much, Jeff. Don't say no to us." Rick's head was on Jeff's shoulder, his hand caressing Jeff's cheek.

"How can I say no to you?"

Rick looked at him. "You can't."

He took Jeff's hand and looked at his tired face. "You ready to talk to Bill. He'll understand, Jeff. I hate to put him in danger when I don't have to, although if I know Bill, he's having a pretty hot time in the Big Easy."

Jeff half smiled. "If you're trying to pull a fast one here, Rick,..." He didn't finish. He didn't know how he would finish.

"If I am, you can spank me," Rick teased, squeezing his butt for Jeff's benefit. Jeff reached down and smacked Rick on his ass.

"Like that?"

"Ouch. I guess so."

Rick walked to the kitchen and picked up his cell phone. "I'm going to call him right here, so that you will be able to hear everything, okay?" Jeff nodded. It took four rings before Bill answered. Rick had almost given up, thinking that Bill had found himself a little too much fun the night before, when he heard his boss' sleepy voice.

"Huh?"

"Bill?"

"Yeah, Rick."

"Were you asleep? It's almost noon here, which means it is almost one in the afternoon in New Orleans, buddy."

"Oh, man, send me to a party city, will ya?"

Rick knew how much Bill liked to party, and for a middle aged man, he could keep up with guys half his age.

"Hey, buddy, I need to talk serious now," Rick said.

"Okay, okay," Bill said, trying to focus. He was naked, and he looked around, but, no, he was alone. "Okay, what do you got?"

"Bill, I have a confession."

"Okay, step into my confessional," Bill joked.

"No, Bill, seriously."

"Okay, okay, I couldn't resist."

Rick told his boss everything and then asked to put him on the speaker so that Jeff could hear. Bill had seen just about everything in his years with the agency, so he wasn't too shocked, at least. "So, you sent me down here to get my ass kicked for nothing," he said.

Rick hoped he was joking. "Uh, no, Bill. I didn't want that at all."

"Well, that's okay, Rick. But, I did get laid last night."

Jeff couldn't believe that Rick's boss was saying these things.

"Okay, I'll come back. Seriously though, they are reopening the case of Pierre Moran's death. They want to find the body."

Jeff nodded to Rick. "We can help you with that," Rick assured him.

"Jeff, you with us on this?"

"Yes, sir," Jeff answered.

"Well, wait a minute. I wasn't thinking. Jeff will need to come back here to give a statement to the police. No, give me a minute. Have him give the statement to you, and record it. That way we've got a better shot at keeping Jeff safe. Better stay in Denver. I'll be back there tomorrow. Sound good, Jeff?"

"Yes, sir," he said.

Rick hung up the phone after Bill did and looked at Jeff. "Well, what do you think of Bill?"

"I guess I'm surprised that he wants to help. I don't know *how* I feel, Rick."

"Look, Jeff. Things are going to get tough, real tough. I don't have to tell you that. For now, we're going to get you up to the cabin in those mountains you were so impressed with."

"What? Stay there alone?"

"No, Jeff, no. I will be there. I should have said *we*. Both of us. We have used that cabin for many years now, and this can work. This *will* work."

Jeff lay down on the sofa.

"You okay?"

Jeff sighed. "Yeah. I'm just tired, Rick."

Rick walked over and sat down beside him. "Look, Jeff. As soon as we get to the cabin, we'll rest. Right now, though, we've really got to be going. It's about an hour drive. You up to it?"

"Give me a minute and I will be."

Rick left Jeff alone for awhile while he packed enough clothes for both of them. It will be colder up in the mountains, so coats are a definite necessity. "I hope there's enough wood for the fireplace. I'm sure that Jeff has never chopped wood." Fortunately, the cabin was always well stocked with the essentials and plenty of nonperishable foods. It's a long way to the nearest anything up there.

Jeff was leaning on the side of the door when Rick turned around. "Ready to go?"

"Sure," he said, looking at the man who was willing to risk his life for him.

Jeff just sighed. He picked up a pile of the clothes.

"Let's set them on the sofa for now, Jeff. We don't want anyone to see you. I will pull the car into the garage first, and then you can get into the vehicle without going outside."

Jeff nodded and took the clothes to the living room.

Bill gathered his two bags and hailed a taxi from downtown New Orleans to the airport. "Hey, buddy, you don't look so good." The cabbie helped him with his bags. "Oh, this is not the place for me," Bill admitted, and laughed at his own hung over condition. "I like to party and I like sex, and this city has too much of both for a junkie like me." Bill laughed at himself again.

"I know what you mean. Boy, do I know." The driver laughed with Bill.

"Oh, I feel like something the cat wouldn't even bother to drag in," Bill went on.

They got to the airport, and the driver helped Bill with his bags. "Well, take care, buddy. Come back and see us sometime."

Bill laughed at the man's comment. "I know I shouldn't, but I probably will." Bill could feel his headache coming on. He needed either very strong coffee or another drink. Fortunately, he didn't have to wait long for his plane.

Bill boarded the plane, found his seat, and sat down. Changing his ticket was difficult enough, but he didn't mind being in first class, even if it did cost a little more.

"Oh, hi, how ya doin'?" Bill asked the man seated beside him. The man didn't reply, but continued to sit with his head down, the hood of his sweatshirt covering most of his face. "You must be in about as good of shape as I am," Bill added. Bill decided not to push it. Hell, if the kid doesn't want to talk, I can't force him to, he thought. Bill made himself comfortable and waited for the plane to take off.

They reached cruising altitude and had been in the air just a short while when the man beside Bill tapped him on the leg. "What's this?" The man handed Bill a note and a card of some sort. Bill opened the note.

"Don't say a word. I am Pierre Moran, the one they thought they got rid of. This is my proof, my driver's license. I know another of your agents. He informed me of your flight. I need your help and will do whatever you want."

Bill closed the note and shoved it into his pocket. Then he looked at the card. It was Pierre's license, but was this man Pierre? Pierre slowly turned his head Bill's way and pulled back the hood of his sweatshirt just enough for Bill to see his face. Bill's mouth dropped. Shit, it was him.

Pierre turned back around with his head down and covered by the hood of the sweatshirt.

"No problem," Bill muttered, and Pierre nodded.

Bill had so many questions for this man, but he knew he couldn't ask them here. Who do they think they sunk into the Mississippi River? he wondered.

As the plane descended over Denver, Bill said quietly, "Follow me," and Pierre nodded. Bill got his bags and walked across the parking lot to his car. Once inside the car, Pierre pulled his hood back, but slouched down in the seat. "You look like hell, man," Bill said.

"I feel like hell," he answered.

"Where you been livin'?"

"Alleys, empty warehouses, anywhere. Had hoped to leave with your buddy, Rick. But I guess Jeff is with him."

"That's right, but how did you know?"

"I overheard your conversation. I was hiding inside the hotel ventilation system."

Bill knew that he wasn't kidding about that. He certainly looked like he had been living in a ventilation system. "How did you know the ventilation system enough to find my room?"

"I helped install the system. The family owns the hotel."

"Well, let me think. Rick is taking Jeff to the main cabin, and we can't take you both there. Too much risk."

"Jeff can't know I'm alive, yet."

"I know, Pierre. It's too risky. When things get tough, you would be the perfect pawn for Jeff. What about your wife?"

"Don't you mean widow? That's old news. She should have told me about her family when we first started getting serious. What I felt for her died the night her family had me killed, or thought that they had me killed."

Bill started driving and headed to his home just south of Denver. "About that, *were* you in the cedar chest, or what the hell happened that night?"

"Yeah, I was in there, but Sammy and JoJo aren't the sharpest knives in the drawer, if you know what I mean. They forgot that I knew how the 'special' cedar chests were made. They were stupid enough to use one of them for me. And they were stupid enough to believe that I was dead, when I really had just faked being knocked out by them. I know exactly where and how to not take a punch. Anyway, there's a breakaway part on the bottom of the cedar chests that is just big enough to barely fit through. The family uses them for transporting things they might need to unload quickly, if you get my drift here. That's how they've been able to stay just a few steps ahead of the feds, so far at least."

Bill thought this was wild. He loved hearing about the "magic" of the families.

"Anyway, I was in pretty bad shape and it took all the energy I had just to stay underwater long enough and swim far enough away from where they had forced me underwater, to make it all the way back to the top. By the time I made it back up, I was far enough from where the cedar chest had been pushed into the river that Sammy and JoJo could no longer see me. They had already gone anyway, Sammy and JoJo. They're big, but not all that bright."

"Wow," Bill said. "That's like something straight out of the movies."

"A horror movie," Pierre said. "Anyway, I've been living off my wits since then. When your buddy Rick left New Orleans, I thought my chances of getting out of there for good were slim."

Bill sighed. "Well, here we are," he said, and pulled into the drive. "Come on in and we'll figure something out."

When Rick and Jeff reached the cabin, it was snowing lightly. "Oh, my God, that's snow," Jeff exclaimed.

"Sure is, and it's only going to come down harder and get deeper. That's what makes this place a good hideout. Hard to get up here."

They walked inside and Jeff looked around. It was cozy, but even smaller than Rick's house. The living room was small, with a kitchenette attached. "Look at this view!"

"It's pretty," Rick answered.

"It's gorgeous, Rick. I love the mountains. This is like a Normal Rockwell painting."

"Haven't seen much snow, huh?"

"No. Just when we'd go to Kansas in the winter for a few days, but we didn't do that very often."

Rick walked up behind Jeff and put his arms around him. "It's even more beautiful when someone points it out to me, someone who doesn't see it every day." He kissed Jeff's neck.

"So, how safe am I here, really?"

"We've got all the best and the finest up here, invisible bodyguards, weapons, bugged phones, and a couple of real bodyguards in that building back there." Rick pointed to an even smaller cabin not far from them.

"I don't know, Rick. It's still going to be tough keeping ahead of my family."

Rick was too busy unbuttoning Jeff's shirt and kissing the back of his neck to pay too much attention to what he was now saying.

Jeff pulled Rick around, almost knocking him off of his feet, and helped him to the floor. Jeff got on the floor with his knees on either side of Rick and leaned over him.

"What are you going to do with me?" Rick tried to act frightened.

"Whatever I feel like doing," Jeff informed him. He leaned down, and being careful not to touch Rick with his hands, he leisurely ran his tongue along Rick's lips. Rick tried to reach up and pull him down, but he couldn't. "Mm, you taste good," Jeff teased, not giving in to Rick.

"Get a bigger taste," he offered Jeff.

Jeff opened Rick's shirt and his lips moved to that bigger taste offered by Rick, the taste of Rick's nipples. With Rick's arms held to his sides by Jeff, he could barely move them. He was held captive by Jeff's lips on his hard nipples. The scent of Jeff's hair and the feel of it against his chest were causing Rick's jeans to tighten against his burgeoning erection. Jeff moved down and swirled his tongue around and then in Rick's navel. Rick hoped that Jeff freed his hard cock soon before he broke the zipper in his jeans.

Jeff stripped his own shirt off, and then he placed Rick's hands on his nipples and arched his back. "Touch me, Rick," he said, and Rick circled the big nipples, ran his fingers over them lightly, and then harder, and finally, pinching them lightly between his fingers.

Rick looked at Jeff's tight jeans and didn't wait for an invitation. He quickly unzipped them and lowered them as much as he could, grabbing for the hardness within and pulling it out.

He pushed Jeff's shorts down as far as he could, stroking his thick manhood and reaching in further for those heavy balls that were filled with the sweet cream that Rick would soon have.

Jeff couldn't wait any longer. He lifted up so that Rick could push his jeans down, and Jeff quickly stripped them off. He undid Rick's jeans and then stripped them off, too. Jeff straddled Rick, and their cocks felt good together. They watched as their two hard rods played, their drops of pre-cum mixing together. Jeff held their cocks together in his hands, stroking the shafts, pulling them slowly upward.

Rick watched this erotic scene, and then Jeff surprised him. He leaned down and laid his tongue flat over the top of both cocks and slid it across them. "Oh, damn, Jeff," he moaned. Rick put his hands around Jeff's hands, and ran his fingers across the top of the two cocks. Jeff closed his eyes, but then quickly opened them again. He didn't want to miss a minute of this erotic scene. "Help me up," Rick said to his lover. Jeff helped him sit up.

Rick ran his tongue across the top of both cocks while Jeff watched. "See what you did to me when *you* did this?" "Damn," was all that Jeff could say. Rick pushed him backward. "Give me that hard tasty thing," he said, and grabbed Jeff's dick. He held it up, and then licked up and down the shaft, and then all the way around, stopping when he reached the top, and then he looked at Jeff. "Watch, Jeff," he said. Jeff opened his eyes and watched as Rick licked the top of his cock several times. Then he held the swollen head of Jeff's cock between his lips, and Jeff watched as it disappeared.

Jeff was hot now, hot for Rick. He sat up, grabbed Rick's ass, spun him around and forced his legs apart. Rick kept Jeff's cock inside his mouth and grabbed onto Rick's legs. "I'm hungry, Rick. Feed me." Rick lowered his ass and moved around so that Jeff had to wait for his cock to meet his lips. Rick teased him by dangling his cock just out of reach of Jeff's mouth. Jeff licked the top as Rick's hard cock circled around, and then he grabbed Rick's balls hard and forced the teasing treat down and into his mouth. "Oh," Rick moaned, as the warmth of Jeff's mouth forced him to be still for a minute from its intensity. Jeff was going at it so good that it was hard for Rick to continue. He slowly began to tease Jeff's cock with his tongue, going all the way down until Jeff's cock was all the way in his mouth, until he could swipe his tongue across Jeff's balls. Jeff moaned. Rick squeezed Jeff's thighs as he held on, not wanting to climax yet.

They wanted each other even more than they had ever thought possible. They pulled with their mouths and sucked the drops from the top of each other's cock, eager for the explosive climax they were both nearing. Jeff thrust his cock hard into Rick's mouth, and Rick's balls slammed against Jeff's chin, until at last they moaned that low deep growl that came just seconds before the big explosion. They fed each other their cum as they realized their own orgasm.

Rick lay against Jeff's leg, and Jeff held Rick's softening dick inside his mouth and squeezed Rick's butt that was so gorgeous and right in front of him. He slid a finger along the crack that was wide open and begging for attention. "Hey, save some for later," Rick teased. "Mm," Jeff answered.

They reluctantly got up and they realized they had been in front of the glass window the entire time.

"Oh, man, Rick. If those mountains could talk."

Rick looked out at the snow. "We could have entertained some winter hikers. Hikers are a rare sight this far up with the threat of heavy snow imminent, but it could have happened. I think they would have gotten a damn good show."

The phone rang, and Rick answered it as he pulled his jeans on. "Bill, you back already?"

"Yeah, buddy. Think I'll stay in the cabin down the road from you for a few days, kinda lay low."

"That's probably a good idea, Bill. Weather's a bit rough up here. Take it easy."

"I will, Rick, thanks. I'll be in touch."

Jeff heard everything that Rick had just said to his boss. "Is he coming here?"

"No, Jeff, but he'll be only about a mile from here. We have another cabin. Don't know if he'll stop by, but I wouldn't be surprised." Jeff looked nervous.

"Bill isn't going to blow your cover, Jeff. He's to close to his goal. Bill has been trying to stop "The Bayou Boys" for a long time."

"Is that what you call us?"

"That's what my boss came up with. You'd like him, Jeff. Bill is something else, that's for sure."

"He sounds pretty cool. You two ever hook up?"

Rick took a deep breath. "No, we didn't. There was a time about six years ago when we were both in between relationships and we kinda flirted with the idea, but we're really better at being good friends."

"Friends with benefits?"

"No, Jeff, just friends."

"Any regrets?" Jeff was curious about Rick's past.

"No, none. But seriously, Jeff. Don't worry about Bill. He's true blue, solid gold, what you see is what you get." Rick smiled, and Jeff was beginning to feel at least a little more comfortable with his situation.

"You really think this will work?"

"I sure do, Jeff," he said. "Let's unpack and settle in."

"Well, looks like we're going to the mountains, Pierre," Bill announced. "Help me pack some clothes for you. My buddy, Rick, says it's snowing and it might be rough going."

"Sure, Bill," he said and followed Bill's lead. "Think I got time for a quick shower?"

"Sure, Pierre, but make it quick okay? Last I heard on the news, your case is being reopened. Guess your wife heard that there was no body found. Your dad tried to talk her out of having the case reopened but couldn't press it too hard without blowing his own secret."

Pierre just stared at him. "Damn, girl's got some balls. If that had been anybody else asking questions or showing suspicion, the old man would have made sure that a nice snack was made of them for the gators in the swamps."

"So, Pierre, are you sure you're up to all of this, now that your wife is obviously missing you?"

"That's ex-wife now, Bill. And nothing has changed. Ten years of the paranoia, always watching my back, doing the right thing, going to her dad's every Sunday for brunch, stepping to whatever his tune was all the time, were enough for me, too much for me. And you can see what happened with just one misstep."

Bill studied Pierre's face. "Why did they want you dead, Pierre? All I know is that the family thought that you were trying to be the 'boss'."

"Oh, so that's their story. I should have known. That's how paranoid they are, Bill. The truth is, my brother who is also an attorney, agreed to represent a customer of the Giaconi family who didn't receive all the goods he had been promised by Giaconi Furniture. Well, Lucian insisted that he had sent them all, but he had been drinking and did not fill the order completely. All he would have had to do was send the rest of the shipment, but not Lucian. No one challenges the great Lucian Giaconi. He made a fake purchase order for the few items that the customer actually did receive, to give the appearance that the few items actually *was* the original order, and then he killed my brother, or had him killed, rather. He was killed in order to send a message to other customers that Lucian was always right, and that the customer was never to question him."

"So, how and when did you get involved?"

"I told Cheri what I thought about the situation, too, and that her dad should admit that he's not perfect," Pierre said.

"So obviously she told her dad what I had said or I wouldn't be here now, although I'm glad that I am. But that's why I definitely do not want her back."

Bill understood now, and he was right about Lucian. "Never lose Lucian", he was called.

Bill and Pierre made it to the cabin just as the snow started to pile up. "This is going to be a big one," Bill said, looking out at the ominous looking clouds.

"Is there always this much snow here?"

"Pretty much, at least in the winter."

"Reminds me of my grandparents' home in northern France, but I haven't been there since I was a very young boy."

"Well, that's one place I have never been, Pierre. Been to lots of countries, but never France."

The driving was getting pretty treacherous by the time they reached the cabin. "Damn, it's cold in here," Bill said, as he brought their things in. "I left New Orleans for this?"

He looked at Pierre. "Kick the heat on for me," Bill said.

"Gladly."

The heater started right up and Bill started a fire in the fireplace. "It won't take long in a cabin this small to warm up in here. I'll make us some coffee."

"Thanks, Bill."

The place was warm in no time.

"Well, guess you should know. We're helping another guy get out of organized crime and he and my buddy, Rick, are about a mile down the road. We have all kinds of special equipment to detect intruders, although it isn't visible, so don't worry. Just wanted you to know."

"Oh, what family is he with? Maybe I've heard of him."

Bill didn't look at Pierre. He had no idea what he would think if he knew that Jeff Giaconi was just down the road. If it were me, I'd want to go and tear him apart, Bill thought. "Now that you know that my buddy is just down the road, I can give him a quick call. Hard not to hear everything in these tiny cabins."

Bill dialed Rick's number. "Hey, Bill, you made it."

"Yeah, we're here. Looks like we've got a big storm ahead of us, though."

"We sure do. Listen, buddy, the heater went out over here and we're not having much luck with the fireplace."

"Well, what can we do?" Rick knew what Bill was referring to. Could they take the chance of Pierre and Jeff meeting? Rick and Bill were both silent for a few minutes.

"Well, can't have you freezing. Come on over."

Rick trusted Bill's judgment, so they packed they stuff and headed out to meet up with Bill and Pierre.

When they parked outside, Jeff asked, "So, I guess your boss is doing the same thing you are, I mean, stashing someone."

"That's right." Jeff couldn't wait to see who it was, or if he had heard of the person. He loved a mystery.

They walked inside and Bill looked nervous to Rick, which Rick found odd. Bill was always very sure of himself and quite composed. Jeff didn't see anyone else, so he introduced himself to Bill. "I'm Jeff," he said.

Pierre heard the voice and came charging down the short hallway. He headed right for Jeff, poised to kill. "You bastard, you son of a bitch, you fucking bastard. You had me killed."

Bill and Rick both had to pull him off of Jeff. "Bill, what the fuck?"

"Okay, okay, let's stop for a minute, truce, guys."

Rick looked at his boss with a worried and somewhat disgusted look. Who was this guy threatening Jeff? he wondered.

Jeff recovered himself, and stared at Pierre. "How?"

"How am I alive, how did I survive, why am I not dead like you wanted?"

Jeff was immediately on the defensive. "Look, you know who ordered your 'removal' and you know it wasn't me. And, you know who carried it out, too."

Bill and Rick were still holding Pierre, but he was beginning to calm down. "You are not blameless or guilt-free, my former brother-in-law."

"You're right, but I've tried twice before to leave the family, or don't you remember?"

Pierre looked shocked. "No you didn't."

"You lied and said you would help me one of those times, right after your wedding, and you saw me after the family's 'reminders', didn't you?"

"They told me you got beat up by another family," Pierre said honestly.

No one said anything for awhile. Pierre did not know about Jeff's other attempt to leave the family, nor about the 'reminders' from the family when he was forcibly returned. "I didn't know, Jeff."

"I thought you did, Pierre. You going back to Cheri?"

Then Jeff turned pale and he began to sweat. Bill continued to hold Pierre away from Jeff, and Rick went to Jeff and helped him lie down on the sofa. Rick sat on the floor beside Jeff. "I'll kill you, Pierre, before you ever have a chance to tell the family you saw me here."

"You dumbass, Jeff. They want me dead. Why would I give them proof that I was alive?"

Jeff closed his eyes.

Rick broke in. "Okay, guys, you both want out of the family or you wouldn't be here."

"How did you get here, Pierre?" Jeff wanted to know.

"Sammy and JoJo aren't very bright. They put me in one of the family's 'special' cedar chests. I broke out the bottom and barely made it to the top of the river before I really did drown. I hid out in warehouses and ate out of trash cans until I finally got my big break."

Bill filled in the rest for Rick.

Pierre sat down and looked at Jeff. He looked like a beaten man. He didn't look like that poised member of the family that he had seemed all these years. He tried to think back to the times when Jeff had supposedly been beaten by another family. He leaned his head back and closed his eyes.

Rick and Bill looked at each other. Pierre and Jeff had cleared a few things up, but they still shouldn't be staying together.

Bill went down the hall and into the only bedroom in the small cabin, and closed the door. He called another member of the agency to see if there were any other cabins or other hideaways that were unoccupied at this time. He came back and told Rick that he and Jeff should stay up here in the mountains.

"They think they did away with Pierre, so he and I will go down to Colorado Springs. They've got one small house there that isn't occupied."

"It's pretty bad outside. The snow is coming down fast, Bill," Rick said, worried for his boss, but not wanting to share the cabin with anyone but Jeff.

"We'll make it. Come on, Pierre."

Bill winked at Rick on their way out. He understood, and there certainly wasn't any reason for Pierre to know *everything* about his brother-in-law.

After Bill and Pierre had left, Jeff looked at Rick. "Damn, Rick, I had no idea. He's the key, Rick."

"I know, Jeff. I was just as shocked as you, and so was Bill when he first saw him. He was sitting next to Bill on the plane, and Bill was so hung over he thought he was hallucinating." Rick laughed when he thought of Bill's reaction.

"How can we know what's going on with Pierre's case in New Orleans way up here in a cabin in the mountains, Rick?"

"Right here," he said.

Rick took out his laptop and fortunately was able to connect through wireless Internet. "Yes, it works up here," he exclaimed. He sat on the floor and Jeff rolled onto his side. "Looks like the reopened case made national headlines."

Jeff was intrigued. He didn't know his sister had it in her, but she was determined to know what happened to the body of her husband, even if it meant going against her father. "Oh, my God, Rick," he said, as they watched.

The authorities in New Orleans had dragged the Mississippi River for Pierre's body and had uncovered the cedar chest. In it were some of Pierre's personal effects. "He left those on purpose, Rick. I just know it. Damn." Jeff was impressed. Pierre's watch, wedding ring, and parts of the shirt that he had obviously torn off before breaking out of the cedar chest had been found inside the chest. "Sammy and JoJo are dead men walking now, that's for damn sure." Jeff laughed. "Serves them right, though. You probably guessed that they were the ones who beat the shit out of me, twice." Yes, Rick had suspected. "Dad must be so pissed right now, and maybe just a little bit scared," Jeff said, with satisfaction.

They continued to watch as the Feds discovered the opening in the bottom of the cedar chest. "Cheri doesn't even know about the special cedar chests, Rick. None of the women do. It's top secret, trust me. Dad holds that secret very tight. The old man must be shittin' his pants."

Rick was glad to see Jeff upbeat, even if it was in this weird situation. Rick was used to this kind of life. After they got the latest news, Jeff asked, "So, what comes next, Rick?"

"Well, thanks to the investigation, our job is a lot easier now. When Bill decides to, he and a small army of federal agents will show up in New Orleans with your supposed "dead" brother-in-law and he can tell them everything that happened to him. By then, you and I can be long gone, if you want to be. I can work from anywhere, Jeff. You, however, will have to change your identity and maybe your looks somewhat."

"I won't have to go back?"

"Not now that they have Pierre to blow the lid off the entire operation. You can make a statement from here. I'll have to talk to Bill to be sure about that, but I think that Pierre's return from the dead will be enough to put them away."

Jeff still doubted that Pierre's return would stop his dad from doing his business as usual. Besides, he never actually killed anyone himself, he ordered others to kill, and Pierre couldn't prove that Lucian had been the one who had ordered his death.

"What about your sister, Jeff?"

"Oh, she'll expect Pierre to come running back to her, but he won't, and why the hell would he? He's got family in France. I really expect him to return to his home land."

Rick noticed something in Jeff's face then, confusion, doubt, but something. "What is it, Jeff?"

"Dad will still get off somehow. They can't prove he murdered anyone, and Pierre is alive."

"But Pierre did confess right here that your father tampered with an invoice, didn't he?"

Jeff sat up. "Yes, he did, and I think the sale was part of a government contract."

Rick smiled. "You think Pierre remembers that, and which one?"

"Not sure. You might want to check on that, Rick. Pierre's been through a lot."

Rick waited until he thought that Bill should have made it to Colorado Springs, giving him an extra hour due to the bad weather, and called his cell phone.

"Bill, you make it there yet?"

"Just walked in, buddy. Boy, that was some storm. Got a much bigger place here, though. Well worth the drive. What's up?"

"Jeff has just informed me that the invoice discovered by Pierre's brother was part of a government contract."

"Great. I'll jog Pierre's memory on this. That should help a lot. They might be good at covering their murder tracks, but tampering with a government invoice, or tax evasion, or the like, gets them every time." "Well, keep in touch, buddy," Bill added, and then was gone.

Jeff turned to Rick. "Do you really think there is a possibility that I might not be on the run for the rest of my life?"

Rick sat down beside him. He thought about it for several minutes. "I do, Jeff. A lot of things are in your favor here. Pierre is at much greater risk because they needed him out of the way, even more than I had originally realized, but with your statement and Pierre's return from the dead, this is a much different case than my usual crime family mystery."

"Mind if I lie down for awhile, Rick?"

"Not at all, Jeff. You're tired, right. You're not sick?"

"No, just tired."

While Jeff slept, Rick got out his laptop and documented all that had transpired over the last couple of days.

Rick and Jeff remained in the little cabin for two weeks before heading back to Rick's home in Denver. They met secretly with Bill and Pierre under the cloak of darkness every day at an undisclosed location between Denver and Colorado Springs, as they prepared for Pierre's return to New Orleans.

Bill had obtained a copy of both the original as well as the "tampered with" invoice which Pierre's brother had had the good foresight to have filed with the appropriate governmental agency.

This one act of fraud and Lucian's inability to provide evidence to refute it were enough to arrest the elusive crime boss.

Bill and Pierre prepared to return to New Orleans for what promised to be a great show, Pierre Moran's return from the dead. Jeff and Pierre understood each other now, if not yet able to fully trust each other. "Take care, buddy," Jeff told him. They shook hands, and Pierre and Bill flew out of Denver to return to New Orleans. Jeff had provided Bill with his official statement which would also no doubt cause raised eyebrows among the family.

It was late October when the trial began and was shown on every major network. The knowledge that no body had been found in Pierre's presumed death intrigued the nation.

Rick and Jeff had opened a bottle of wine and had filled a tray with as many different kinds of chocolate they could find and had settled in on the sofa for the moment they had been waiting for, the return from the dead of Pierre Moran.

Rick handed a glass of wine to Jeff, poured a glass for himself, and set the bottle on the table beside him. He took Jeff's hand and held it in his. "You sure you're ready for this? We don't have to watch."

"Are you kidding? I wouldn't miss this for the world," Jeff assured him, stuffing his mouth with a handful of the delicious chocolates.

The prosecutor asked how Pierre Moran had died, and no one seemed to know. Lucian denied knowing anything about the possibility of murder, and Sammy and JoJo each had blackmailed a friend to provide them an alibi for their whereabouts the night of Pierre's death. "Why was the body never seen by Mrs. Moran?" the prosecutor asked.

Lucian seemed like the devoted father when he responded. "I couldn't let my little Cheri see his body. It was apparent to us that Mr. Moran had had too much to drink that night and had swerved off the road, landing in the Mississippi River. I didn't want Cheri to know about her husband's drinking problem."

Jeff looked at Rick. "He's a damn good actor, my father, don't you think?"

Rick just smiled. The man was a good actor.

Everyone looked confused when the prosecutor announced the next witness. "The prosecution calls Pierre Moran to the stand." Gasps were heard throughout the courtroom, and no doubt across the nation, and several seconds passed before the doors to the courtroom opened.

Pierre walked in with two federal agents on either side of him and Bill behind him. Lucian's mouth dropped, and so did every other family member's, along with those of a very intrigued nation watching from their homes.

As Pierre prepared to take the stand, Cheri recovered from her shock and ran up to him. "You're alive. I knew you weren't dead. Oh, I've missed you so much."

Pierre stopped her short. "Do not touch me, bitch."

She was led back to her seat in tears, and Pierre told his story.

"Wow," Jeff repeated several times during Pierre's recounts of his life with the Giaconi family.

Pierre told everything and described in great detail the breakout bottoms of the "special" cedar chests. Lucian didn't flinch. It was as if the man were made of stone. When asked if he were supposed to have been murdered, Pierre began to say that his death had been ordered, but the defense stopped him, for awhile.

Jeff's lengthy statement was read, and watching it Jeff held tighter to Rick's hand. He could see by the look in his father's face that he knew he had been beat this time.

When they scanned the courtroom, Rick caught sight of Bill. "Man, he is lapping this up. He loves the kill."

Jeff smiled. Bill did look happy, and maybe just a little hung over.

"Looks like he picked up where he left off the last time he was in the Big Easy, doesn't it?" Rick laughed at his own assessment.

"Sure does," Jeff agreed.

"The man does like to party." Rick laughed again.

When asked the whereabouts of his son, Jeff Giaconi, Lucian said that he did not know the whereabouts of his son, but very few believed him.

"Is he dead?" the prosecutor asked.

"I do not know the whereabouts of Jeff Giaconi," Lucian icily responded.

"That's good, Jeff. Not knowing if you are alive or dead is in your favor. But, one thing is pretty clear. Unfortunately, you can't go home."

Jeff looked at Rick. "I am home, Rick. I am home."

This print book is available in ebook form from the following:

Apple iBookstores

Barnes & Noble

Amazon Kindle Stores

Kobo ebooks

Rainbow ebooks

Sony Reader Store

All Romance ebooks

Bookstrand

Coffeetime Romance